TALADOR STRUCK...

. . . lightning swift, made his roundup and hardly even slackened pace, speeding away as suddenly as he'd arrived.

Ben and Jeff wasted only a moment at the canvas-camp, then punched their mounts into a lope and headed warily on up the riverside to the area where the mules had been serenely grazing the last time either man had seen them.

There was not a mule. Not a single one, anywhere. . . . Jeff jumped to earth, flung his reins over a branch, drew his Colt, and plunged ahead into the darkness of the twisted willow-growth . . .

D1513464

OTHER ACTION-PACKED WESTERN ADVENTURES
FROM DELL

THE MAN IN BLACK *by Al Conroy*
ROPE THE WIND *by Norman A. Fox*
RED GRASS *by Carter Travis Young*
NAVAJO CANYON *by Tom W. Blackburn*
HOME TO TEXAS *by Todhunter Ballard*
LAST TRAIN TO BANNOCK *by Al Conroy*
THE DERBY MAN *by Gary McCarthy*
SHORT GRASS *by Tom W. Blackburn*
SHOWDOWN AT SNAKEGRASS JUNCTION
by Gary McCarthy
BUCKSKIN MAN *by Tom W. Blackburn*
DIL DIES HARD *by Kelly P. Gast*
LONG LIGHTNING *by Norman A. Fox*
LONG WAY TO TEXAS *by Lee McElroy*
LOCO *by Lee Hoffman*

THE KIOWA PLAINS

Frank Ketchum

A DELL BOOK

Published by
Dell Publishing Co., Inc.
1 Dag Hammarskjold Plaza
New York, New York 10017

© Robert Hale Limited 1978

All rights reserved.
For information address St. Martin's Press, Inc.,
New York, New York.

Dell ® TM 681510, Dell Publishing Co., Inc.

ISBN 0-440-14809-X

Reprinted by arrangement with St. Martin's Press, Inc.

Printed in the United States of America

First Dell printing—October 1979

THE
KIOWA PLAINS

1

HILL AND HURLEY

They came up out of Mexico through the Province of Sonora and entered Arizona at the border town of Nogales which was more Mex than American, and after that they at least had a countryside to pass through where people spoke English.

Both Ben Hurley and Jefferson Hill understood Spanish; at least they could get along passably well in border-Mex, which had its basis in Spanish but which was also liberally laced with Indian words and a sort of border-country colloquial lingo no real Spaniard could have made heads or tails of.

But the relief freighters felt when they got up across the line and above Nogales had little to do with anyone's inability to carry on much of a conversation south of the border. It had a whole lot more to do with *gringo* law and order which was vigorously enforced by not just local marshals and possemen and constables, but was also enforced by army patrols and U.S. Marshals. The farther freighters went from Nogales northward, the less chance they had of being raided.

Which did not mean they would not be robbed; it simply meant that the chances were less that it would happen, and in a territory where the only two constants were heat and poverty, there were probably very close to being as many outlaws above the border as below it—except that above it they were far more likely to be captured or killed.

Sometimes the distinction seemed difficult to define, or to pin down, but to freighters like Jeff Hill and Ben Hurley it was nevertheless a great relief to see Nogales dead ahead, and eventually to wheel right on up through it back up into Arizona.

Freighting was not usually something people fell over each other to attempt, and only a very few freighters would take on a load below the line, or deliver one down there. Also, there were at least three other factors freighters could not avoid but which many other people not only could avoid, but could readily ameliorate. One of them was the heat. In lower and central Arizona, or New Mexico, or even Texas for that matter, summertime never arrived shyly and spread a gentle, benign tender warmth, it arrived straight out of the opened gates of Hades, curled the grass, dehydrated the animals, sweated men down to sinew and leathery-brown hide, and hung on sometimes up into November and December.

Freighters had to drive through that kind of heat regardless, and because they rarely reached areas where tree-shade could be found, at least in the desert country of southern Arizona, they had to rumble along into worlds of shimmering, dancing, hazy heat.

And in wintertime, although that particular season

was extraordinarily short on the desert, they also had to drive through frost and biting cold winds which were usually accompanied by sand.

And finally, there were the Indians. Few freight out-fits which had been on the trail very long did not have either old arrow-shafts sawed off flush with their thick wooden sides, or little round holes where bullets and an occasional musketball had embedded itself.

But these were not the Apaches of Nanà's time, or the reservation-jumpers who followed such trouble-makers as old Geronimo or equally as treacherous Escobedo. Those old-time bronco-bucks had been swept away years back. The current Apaches—and some were Mexicans or Comanches, or even a few renegade white masquerading as Apaches—in relation to their forerunners, were as sophisticated as the best renegades usually were. For example, they did not live at White Sands or San Carlos. In fact they did not live on reservations at all. They had a dozen differ-ent secret canyons where they lolled in shady camps trading horses, buying and selling stolen weapons from one another, planning additional raids, and eating bet-ter than their forefathers had ever eaten—from cases of raided tinned foods.

They seldom dressed as Indians, although mostly they continued to wear the ubiquitous *n'deh b'keh* moccasin. They were as likely to suddenly appear firing Colts and Winchesters and riding big strong American horses, wearing bowler hats or soldier caps, or even the singularly-knotted Apache headband, as well as frock coats, or Mexican *vaquero* jackets, or silk shirts with elegant violet-coloured sleeve-garters.

All the impedimenta 'liberated' during those sudden and very murderous raids they launched, would show up later at another site upon one of the howling, gun-firing raiders who became as much a scourge on the desert as their forefathers had been.

Every freighter had encountered these murderers at one time or another, and the moment they reached a town they reported either their bloody encounter or their visual sighting so that the army could rush forth and give chase. But very rarely were the Apaches still out there. In this aspect they were identical to their forerunners. They could fade into the hazy distance more quickly and with better expertise than anyone else, and their scouts were tireless. For either the army or any of the vigilante groups who went Apache-hunting to locate a band on the move, and to approach within gunrange of it, was next to impossible, and for the best trackers serving the army—usually also Apaches—to find their secret places, had happened so rarely most people believed it had never happened at all.

Freighters were their particular prey. Freight wagons were normally weighted with their transportable tonnage, which ensured they could not travel fast. Also, they had to travel the territory, if they were to make deliveries and remain in business. And freight outfits were vulnerable. Usually drawn by at least six horses or mules—oxen had been abandoned some years back as just too slow, even though they were cheaper to purchase and easier to maintain than either horses or mules—but the kind of rigs most freighters used, especially if they traversed hilly country, had as many as ten hitches, or even more; twenty mules or horses, or even more.

The wagons were high-sided and those made in Missouri years back had rear tyres nearly a foot across, and the reason for that was so that laden wagons would not sink into the sand of the south desert country. The more modern rigs had narrower wheels, were never loaded as heavily as were the old Missouri rigs, and could not, because they were smaller, carry as much, but also, they were faster, and that had become increasingly important to people who ordered merchandise to be delivered: speed.

Even so, speed and freighters were about as synonymous as night and day or black and white. The fastest big wagon rarely ever moved out of a flat-footed walk. Neither the hitches nor the wagons themselves were lashed up to make haste, and if the rigs were high-enough-sided, only a fool tried to get up a trot on the downhill grades because those high wagons were also top-heavy and susceptible to toppling over.

There would certainly, eventually, be better methods devised for the delivery of freight, but for about fifty years nothing, neither fast express outfits nor pack-trains, could begin to serve the requirements of all the little villages, towns and *pueblos* of New Mexico and Arizona Territories, with the ponderous, dogged, massive efficiency of freight outfits.

The way Ben Hurley had once explained it to some soldiers he and Jeff met out in the middle of nowhere with surveying instruments, if the government had millions to waste and sent army engineers into the south desert to plot out the course for an eventual railroad, the result would be a freighting-fee no one could possibly afford, because in summertime the railroad would have to keep water-carts moving back and forth soaking wooden ties or they would shrink under the fierce heat and pull away from the steel tracks, or, in wintertime, they would also have to keep crews moving up and down the line constantly, uncovering tracks which were completely covered with sand and wind-blown tons of tan soil.

But Ben also agreed that there had to be a better way to move freight than from the high seat above a giant old wagon, staring at the undulating rumps of twenty mules. But, he told the army surveyors, trying to create a system for that purpose while overlooking all the basic shortcomings of the desert, sure as hell would never be the solution.

Finally, when he and Jeff wheeled up into Madison-ville that same springtime, they were solemnly in-formed that there were seven dead soldiers out back of the doctor's shack, in his buggy shed, killed in their sleep and stripped of everything from their boots to their shiny brass surveying instruments. Ben clucked and told his partner they had neglected to tell those surveyors about that other reason a railroad wouldn't be practical at this time: Apaches.

That was the same summer they delivered thirty sacks of stone-ground flour down into Mexico, and hauled back a hundred well-tanned hides of skirting leather, passed northward through Nogales, and ped-dled most of their hides to several harness-works, along the way up to the green-grass and paloverde country around Lincoln.

Here, they made a camp beside the chocolate Mes-cal River, let the horses and mules drift and rest, worked over their big Missouri wagon, and established a comfortable canvas-camp among the willows and cottonwoods where they strung two lariats from which to drape their laundry, and hauled round stones to create a fire-ring over which to cook.

Big Jeff Hill's inherent good nature surfaced in this place in many ways, and even Ben Hurley's sometimes taciturn stoicism seemed alleviated at the sight and sound of flowing water, at the pleasant shade at riverside, and over the prospect of not having to do a blessed thing he did not care about doing for a while.

They were about a mile above town, which was not too far to walk in, of an evening, for some whisky and poker. It was also just far enough from Lincoln not to have to be concerned about townsfolk.

And they were empty, with no current commitment, for a change. Hurley and Hill were well known throughout lower Arizona. They had never lost a load although they had been raided, and that meant a lot to shippers who did not want to lose their produce very much.

Someone would ride in, sooner or later. As Ben said their third night in camp, the Good Lord did not intend for freighters to rest and relax for very long periods at a time; He had made some men freighters no doubt as a form of penitence; as some kind of punishment because they'd been, maybe, horse-thieves or border-jumpers in a previous life.

Jeff savoured a store-bought cigar and sipped freshly boiled coffee with his long legs shoved out and his otherwise lanky carcass propped against an empty crate, and smiled across the fire at his partner.

"Could have been worse," he suggested. "He could have made us miners, or squatters, or maybe even townsmen who couldn't leave a job in a store or a harness shop or a blacksmith's works." Jeff waved the cigar. "Look at that perfect sky with all those stars and listen to that river. What do you expect from life, anyway?"

Ben pondered a moment before answering. "A rich wife," he said ultimately. "Big and round and with dark eyes and jet-black hair."

Jeff snorted. "You had one of those in Messico last month."

"Not in Mexico," responded his partner. "That's exactly where I don't want her to live." Ben leaned with a bottle in his fist. "Shove out your coffee-cup."

2

TALADOR

Lincoln was a pleasant town. It had genuine trees, planted decades ago by Kansans and Missourians who had settled in the territory near Lincoln to run cattle and horses, and who had never before been in a treeless country.

Lincoln also had several excellent water-wells, also laboriously dug by those same mid-westerners. And it had a tough territorial sheriff named Drake Haslett, a re-settled Texan whose accent was no longer noticeable, but whose Texas-characteristics were inherent. He knew Hurley and Hill. Had in fact known them over at Madisonville when he'd been town constable over there, and that had been seven years earlier.

He rode out to their canvas-camp the third day they had been alongside the Mescal River, and had a cup of coffee in the fresh, early morning with them, and in his own good time got around—Texas-style—to tell them why he had ridden out.

"Raiders cleaned out an old feller named Burns north-east of here maybe four, five miles, couple of days back. He raised horses. They drove all of 'em off but he recovered about six or eight heavy old mares which couldn't keep up. He also found four little colts been shot because they couldn't keep up either. Well . . . the point is, there's been trouble all last winter and into this springtime with a son of a bitch called Talador. I figured you boys had ought to be warned." Drake Haslett sat straight and looked northwards up along the green verge where the horses and mules were complacently grazing.

That look was enough. Haslett did not have to say a thing more than he had already said, so he slouched down again and sipped hot coffee, then set aside the cup to roll and light a smoke as Jeff asked about Talador.

"It means 'destroyer' in Mex," Jeff said, then shrugged. "I think that's what it means, anyway."

Sheriff Haslett exhaled smoke. "That's exactly what it means, and this time a raider chose a name that fits."

"Apache?" asked Ben Hurley, and got a rueful glance from the lawman.

"That's sort of like askin' if the ghost was white or blue. No one's seen Talador. Well; maybe some of the Mexicans out back of town have seen him but you'd stand a better chance of getting snow in August down here than you'd stand of making one of those people talk. They always do that—they always attribute superhuman powers to some lousy In'ian or renegade who has managed to stay alive over a year, and you know how they shy away from getting involved in anything they figure to be superhuman. . . . All I know about Talador is that he goes after horses, mostly, and mules. He don't seem to care about catching travellers and cutting their throats for their money and pocket-watches."

Ben had a question for Haslett. "Where do the horses and mules turn up?"

The sheriff spread his hands, palms earthward. "I got no idea. If I wanted to guess I'd say over the line down in Mexico. But that's a pure guess . . . I can tell you this much, though, for a fact. He's stolen at least sixty head of good horses since last November or December, and now that the weather is good again I'll lay you fifty-to-one odds in new money that the bastard will get more active than ever."

Ben waved an arm. "This is pretty much open country, Drake."

Haslett looked pained. "I know what you're thinking. Let me tell you something: That louse and his band never strike until late at night, and by sunup. . . ."

"Well hell, they leave tracks don't they? They can't really be *fantasmas*, Drake."

Haslett cracked a mirthless smile. "Yeah, they leave tracks. You know what happens to folks who go riding along at a walk with their eyes on the ground studying someone's sign? They get ambushed, that's what." Haslett leaned as Ben offered to refill his tin coffee cup. "That old man named Burns I just mentioned? He went after them over their trail, with two Mex cowboys."

"Talador cleaned 'em out," muttered Ben Hurley.

"The two *vaqueros*—yes. Shot them out of their saddles while they were going through a chaparral thicket, and they got old man Burns too, but he clung to the horse and got the hell away from there."

Haslett grinned. "Care to try your luck?"

They didn't. "What for?" asked Jeff, flinging away coffee-grounds. "It's your chore, Drake, not ours."

Haslett continued to grin. "Yeah. Right up until he hears about those saddle animals of yours out yonder, and those eighteen fine young big mules. Boys, Talador'd ride fifty miles over hot coals to raid a camp like this, with just two fellers in it and all those well-broke critters out yonder, his for the taking."

Ben sighed and eyed the lawman accusingly. "You see," he told his partner. "One place decent enough to camp at—and you see, Jeff? There's always some lousy kill-joy."

Haslett laughed, brushed off dust and arose to his lanky full height. "Don't blame me. I'm just trying to keep you from being cleaned out like the old man was. And I made a special trip out here this morning to do it . . . Tell you what I'd do was I in your boots."

"You would hitch up," stated Ben Hurley, "turn around and head right back down into Mexico."

Haslett pursed his lips while considering this. In the end he shook his head. "No. It may be bad up here around Lincoln, but it's nowhere nearly as bad as it is down there. No; but I'd darn well hitch up and either move in closer to town, or else I'd haul on up clean out of Talador's territory. And you know what else I'd do?"

"What?"

"I'd do it today. Tomorrow morning at the very latest. Boys, maybe Talador's a renegade 'Pache, but it seems to me he knows an awful lot for a rag-head. Meaning I wouldn't be a bit surprised to find out sooner or later that he's got spies among the local greasers. I say that because just too darn many co-incidences happened last winter."

Jeff eyed the lawman. In his mild voice he said,

"Tell me something, Drake. Just what you been doing all winter?"

Haslett did not bat an eye. "I been courting a widow-lady named Sylvia Sansouci. But I also been. . . ."

"What kind of a name is that?" Jeff demanded.

Haslett loftily passed over that. "Never asked, gents, and never cared. She's the prettiest thing you'll ever see."

Ben Hurley, who was not really especially fond of womenfolk, dryly said, "And meanwhile this pepperbelly, or Apache, or whatever he is, robs folks blind and has got half your territory on foot."

Drake Haslett fell momentarily silent and looked as though he were considering this likelihood for the first time. Then he eventually brightened and said, "Why no, not half my territory; maybe a third of it though." Then he laughed. "Your disposition never was any good, Ben. Tell me something, Jeff; how have you put up with him so long?"

"He works harder than I do," replied Jeff Hill. "If I can get him annoyed about something while we're loading, by golly he'll darn near load the whole wagon by himself. Now I'll tell you, Drake, that kind of a partner is hard to get these days."

Two of them laughed and the other one looked rueful but did not make a sound until after he had arisen to also fling coffee-dregs away and to step from beneath the canvas ceiling of their camp to range a look up-country. The mules and horses were cropping feed or drowsing in the new-day warmth. It made a scene any stockman would have enjoyed looking at.

"I don't know," Hurley said, still looking up there. "We just got here, and we only set up camp a couple of days ago. There aren't many other decent places to camp. Mostly, folks have cut down all the trees up the river. We'd have to go all the way up to Agua Caliente —thirty-five miles. And we'd have to strike this camp only three days after we set it up. Drake. . . ."

"I told you not to blame me," stated the Texan. "I was only tryin' to do you boys a favour." Haslett started to amble out where he had left his horse tied to a wagonwheel taller than the horse was. "Say; if you're comin' into town this evening we could maybe work us up a nice game of Pedro, of blackjack, or poker, whatever would be your favour, gents."

"We'll be in," stated Jeff.

They stood by the scarred old huge wagon and watched the lawman depart back down-country in the direction of Lincoln.

"Damn it," stated Ben Hurley. "You see how things turn out? I told you the Lord makes freighters out of folks who been real evil in some other life."

Jeff scratched under his ribs. "Or lawmen. I knew a feller once over in Albuquerque who made a hobby of figures, and he told me the life-span of the average lawman here in Arizona was less than. . . ."

"What did he tell you about freighters?" growled Hurley, rudely interrupting.

Jeff looked down his nose. He did not like being cut off in mid-sentence. "He told me—he said freighters who got initials anywhere close to B. H. usually end up spread-eagled over a rear freighter-wheel, while raiders is lighting a fire on the ground, then they spin the wheel and barbecue him."

Ben looked at his partner. "You been reading those dime novels again." He looked northward again and shook his head. "I want to move this camp about as much as I want to grow another leg. It's pretty here, and it's nice and quiet and peaceful."

"Tranquil," stated Jeff. "As the Mexicans say—right tranquil." He cleared his throat. "Drake Haslett don't just ride out this far on a nice week-day morning to scare the hell out of freighters."

Ben was unconvinced. "You just can't tell about people. Up north where I cowboyed years back, it was sheep. Folks despised sheep and anyone who owned them. Down here, there are folks who got no use for freighters."

Jeff stared. "If you're serious, you've been out in the sun too long." He turned to study their huge old wagon. "We'd ought to get a gallon of oil and do the sides and running gear, and it wouldn't hurt to pull the wheels and see if the leathers is still good."

"Sure," agreed his partner. "I figured that's what we'd do while we were in camp here—but we only been here three days. I figured we'd do all that next week."

Jeff turned. "Then we're not going to move?"

Ben fidgeted, and glared after the diminishing shape of Sheriff Haslett. In the end he avoided a direct answer by saying, "If we rode into town early this evening we could eat at the café, get haircuts and maybe shaves at the tonsorial parlour, then look up Haslett and clean him out at poker."

They went back to the place in among the bushes and trees where they had stretched ropes and had afterwards stretched their canvas to form a ceiling. There were no sides to their canvas-camp. There seldom were in a canvas-camp; just a big, overhead tarp above the clearing where men established their temporary residence.

Jeff was rolling a smoke when he said, "Talador; you know, I think I've heard that name before."

Ben grunted. "They always got to give themselves

some kind of damn-fool name. Why couldn't he just be José or Domingo, or maybe Pancho?"

Jeff assented. "Or some Apache name."

"Naw; you can't pronounce those rag-head names." Ben sank down upon an up-ended box and looked around. It was indeed a comfortable camp. Maybe it seemed especially comfortable to him because he had not been able to look forward to this kind of an interlude of relaxation in two years. "If this 'Pache cleaned out that old horse-rancher," he finally told his partner, "chances are he's still down in Mexico where he peddled his stolen horses . . . We got another three, four days before we got to worry."

Jeff's answer was blunt. "Bull! You're kidding yourself. You know how much we stand to lose if some raider drives off those mules out there?"

"Of course I know," growled Ben Hurley, and slapped his legs as he arose from the box. "All right; in the morning we'll strike camp. Only it'd serve Haslett right if we went in closer to town and turned our livestock loose to graze."

They went down to the river, stripped, bathed, then soaked a long while before climbing out and lying in the hot sunlight to dry off before dressing. It was a wonderfully long and hot and lazy day.

By early afternoon when Jeff went forth to fetch back their pair of saddle-horses, Ben had made a very neat job of cleaning up the camp and getting himself rigged out in his clean trousers and shirt, and he even brushed his hat and robbed some axle-grease from a wagon-hub for his boots. When Jeff returned to pass over a shank and look at his partner, Ben was neater than he had looked in months. Jeff was turning away with the other saddle-animal when he muttered, "Sansouci; what the hell kind of a name is that? Anyway, just because Haslett says she's pretty as a spotted pony don't mean you have to put on your clean shirt and all . . . Did you grease your boots, too?"

"Why don't you just saddle that pin-eared horse of yours," retorted Ben Hurley, "and shut up. Since when is it a crime for a man to get cleaned up?"

Jeff hummed a dolorous song of unrequited love as he cuffed his sorrel gelding and hoisted the blanket and the saddle. They would arrive in town a little earlier than he had thought they would, but that was agreeable to him. As for poker, he was a fair hand at it, but Ben was one of the best he'd ever seen. Evidently Drake Haslett did not know this; no man in his right mind would offer to gamble with someone who was an expert.

They left the camp after a final look around. Up north along the river the mules were now seeking shade to stand a while in drowsy contemplation, and because they were mostly mouse-coloured, they blended very well along the riverbank with the mottled growth and the speckled shadows.

Ben shook his head. He was still not at all pleased about having to leave this place. As they came close to Lincoln he irritably said, "And where is the damned army, when this Talador is raiding around here?"

Jeff did not answer. He did not have to, Ben hadn't asked that question because he wanted or expected an answer.

"Sitting in their stockades somewhere," Ben went on, bitterly. "Polishing their equipment and swapping lies, while some lousy rag-head is turning the countryside upside down."

Jeff pointed. "That's the saloon," he announced. He had not heeded a single word his partner had said.

They rode southward to the liverybarn, first, and

left their animals down there to be cared for, then they crossed to the east side of the wide roadway and strolled back in the direction of the barber shop. First things came first, and since neither of them had been shorn since the previous winter, they needed it now, before they needed a café-cooked supper.

The town was quiet and orderly and peaceful in the afternoon heat. Far northward stood some thick, squatty, dark-looking heavy mountains, and for once there was no intervening heat-haze to obscure them.

3

A NIGHT TO REMEMBER

Someone in town owned an egg-sucking dog. That was unusual but not entirely unheard of. As the barman told Ben and Jeff, when he'd been a lad back in Mississippi his folks had had a black man living in their coach-house who'd taught his dog to live right well off chicken nests—until some unsympathetic neighbour shot him.

"That darned dog could pick up two eggs out'n a nest in his mouth, walk plumb home with 'em without so much as makin' a crack, then he'd set down and eat 'em."

Ben listened politely then said, "What's that got to do with Drake Haslett not bein' in here this evening for poker?"

"I'm getting to that," exclaimed the barman. "Someone here in town's got an egg-suckin' dawg, you see, and folks is raising old Ned. No one's seen him; he's smart as a wolf. He raids around at night, different hen-houses. Drake's been all day trying to figure out whose dog it is. That's why he ain't here this evening."

The barman had to hasten away and care for a demanding cowboy. Ben drank his glass of beer right down to the suds, slammed the glass down and disgustedly said, "Egg-sucking dog! I never heard such a silly darned story in my life!"

Jeff looked around. "You don't believe that?"

"Do you?"

"Why sure. I remember when I was back in. . . ."

"I don't want to hear about it," exclaimed Ben Hurley. "You're goin' to turn out to be as big a liar as that darned barkeep." Ben turned. The room was filling up, and it was in fact a large saloon. In fact at one time, back during the hectic and lurid days of the Indian conflicts this building had been the wash-house for a dragoon detachment stationed in what back in those days was more nearly a trading-post than a village.

On all four walls there were initials, dates, names, and uncomplimentary remarks carved into the log walls by long-gone horse-soldiers. In a later era Lincoln's main saloon would have been thoroughly appreciated as an historical landmark. Unfortunately, twelve years after the night Ben and Jeff were arguing about egg-sucking dogs, the place burned to the ground.

The liquor was excellent. Better in fact than was normally to be expected in Arizona where tastes were more nearly related to thirsts than to appreciation of what was good, and what was bad, liquor.

Ben Hurley was not much of a whisky-drinker. He liked beer and an occasional shot-glass of whisky, but he rarely took more than two glasses of beer and one glass of anything harder.

Jeff was an indifferent drinker; he liked one about

as much as he enjoyed the other, but as a matter of fact he had never developed much of a taste for it, either.

But being in a saloon in a town was never, to most rangemen, the answer to a long-delayed prayer for whisky. It was an excuse to be among their own kind, whether they were riders or freighters, or even horse-thieves and rustlers, as long as folks didn't know which ones were the latter two.

Cowtown saloons were where freighters picked up solid information about the roads ahead, the degrees of peril, even what the weather and the markets might be like. It was also where men from distant cow-camps who perhaps only reached a town once a month, learned the latest news and heard the most splendid gossip.

There were of course, drunks, and providing they did not get mean and nasty, or loudly obnoxious, no one paid them the slightest attention. And even when they became insufferable, providing they did not start trouble with other customers, they were left entirely to the rough mercies of the local lawman.

But this was a week-night—Tuesday, in fact—so most of the patrons were townsmen. There was a sprinkling of cowmen and their riding crewmen, but those would only be from the outfits within cannon-distance of town. Cow outfits lying farther out usually had restrictions allowing their rangemen to go to town only on Saturday night.

Still, limited patronage or not, the big old gloomy log building was pretty nearly full by seven o'clock; there were several card games going, and up at the far end of the room north of the cast-iron old Cannon Heater wood-stove, four men were wagering heavily upon a knife-throwing competition where many years past someone had very expertly drawn or painted a target on a bare space of log wall.

Drake Haslett arrived as Ben and Jeff were on their second beer. He had a bandage on his left forearm under the sleeve, which created a noticeable thickness and as he eased against the bar scowling at the saloon-man for service, Ben and Jeff exchanged a sidelong glance. He must have caught the egg-sucking dog.

No one spoke until Marshal Haslett had renewed himself and had pounded the bartop for a refill, then he turned and said, "Stick to freighting. No matter how dangerous it is or how uncomfortable at times, stick to it."

Ben nodded. He had no intention of not sticking to freighting. When the barman arrived Ben ordered another round for himself and his partner. "You up to a few hands of poker?" he asked, and Haslett looked along the bar before answering.

"I'd rather pitch dice. Whatever I do it's got to be something a man can do with one hand." He held up the bandaged forearm. "In my trade you not only are liable to get hit or kicked or cussed out by your customers, but ever' now and then one of them will also bite you."

They got dice from the barman and went to a round table with a green cloth across it, and with a circular high edge all around. There were chairs, but they had been pushed far back by others, and evidently were never popular at this particular table.

They flipped a coin and Sheriff Drake won. He rolled the first toss, coming up with a point which was eight. He blew on the dice and let fly. His second pitch came up seven. He swore with feeling and allowed Jeff to redeem the dice.

"You boys going to pull out?" he asked Ben while watching Jeff pitch a seven and sweep up the pot.

"In the morning," replied Ben, feeding the kitty with another coin.

"North or south?" asked the lawman, also making his position legal by 'coming in.'

"Don't know," stated Ben, watching his partner wind up and fling the dice.

"If I was in your boots I'd get clean out of Talador's territory," cautioned the lawman. "Plumb away from anywhere he's liable to be . . . You wonder why I'm not out after him right now? I'll tell you why. There is a posse of cowmen and horse-ranchers hell-for-leather on his trail, and I notified the army over at Fort Sheridan."

Jeff rolled another seven and swept in another pot. Ben and Sheriff Haslett exchanged a look, and the next time they tossed coins into the pot they were just circumspect enough to barely keep the game alive.

Ben's thoughts on Drake's explanation were not especially complimentary to the sheriff so he kept them to himself. Maybe it was all right for a lawman to allow others to do what he was being paid to do. Ben just did not happen to think so.

Jeff rolled a nine and swore because he did not think he could make such a point. But he made it and picked up another pot.

When Ben and Drake fed the pot the next time they refrained from talking and put baleful, suspicious looks upon Jeff Hill. Jeff's point that time was five, and the second roll afterwards he pitched a seven.

Haslett scooped up the dice.

"How much reward is there on Talador?" asked Ben Hurley, stopping Drake's arm in mid-fling.

"So far nothing," stated Haslett. "He's just our local

headache. Folks say they never even heard of him before last winter and the law authorities I've wrote to
around the country say the same thing." Drake considered the dice and the table, made his cast, then
also said, "But I'll tell you—he's no more a novice at
his trade than you are at yours. Maybe he used another name somewhere else, but he's sure as hell no
greenhorn."

The roll came up a ten and Jeff widely smiled as he
tossed back the dice.

Drake Haslett wound up and threw—another pair
of boxcars. He took the pot. Before he rolled again he
said, "I figure though, after what he done to Burns
and his Mex riders, folks are going to get fired up and
make up a bounty on his scalp . . . He never killed
before this time, he just rustled and run 'em off."

Drake threw. His point was two. "Snake-eyes," he
groaned, and sure enough his third toss came up
seven. He offered the dice to Ben who took them without comment—but that had been in Ben's view, the
beginning of the 'poisoning' of the dice. Nothing good
was going to happen now until they got another set
of dice. He handed them to Jeff, who turned towards
the bar as Ben leaned and said, "Talador your only
headache, Drake?"

Haslett pondered before replying. "No. I got another one; a bastard named Gorman is sparkin' Sylvia
Sansouci. He's a burr under my saddleblanket."

"Cut him out."

"How, for Chris'sake? He owns a big cow outfit
south of town, employs four riders and drives a top-
buggy with yeller running-gear and red wheels. He
takes her out on moonlight nights in that damned
buggy of his."

Ben turned and watched as his partner started back

with a fresh set of dice. His interest in Drake Haslett's romantic difficulties was absolutely nil. The world was full of problems but in Ben Hurley's view none were likely to be asinine and completely insignificant as those having to do with the sentiments of a romantically-attached man and woman.

A large Mexican walked in from the warm night, halted, looked left and right, then turned and shouldered his way over to the table where Ben was holding a fresh pair of dice ready to make a cast.

"Sheriff," the big Mexican said so sharply it drew Ben's head around. "Sheriff; you know who the men are got that wagon-camp alongside the river north of town?"

Haslett was studying the expression on the big Mexican's face as he nodded his head. "Yeah, I know, Hernan'—it's these gents right here. Why?"

The Mexican looked at Jeff and at Ben. "You just been set afoot," he said in accentless English.

Ben's grip on the dice curled and tightened until the dice were biting painfully into his flesh. "What did you say?" he softly enquired.

Jeff walked up from the lower end of the table, to lean and stare at the Mexican.

Drake Haslett introduced the big Mexican. "This here is Hernando Salazar. He rides for Swan Cattle Company north-east of town across the river a couple of miles."

Neither Ben nor Jeff acted as though they had heard a word of the introduction. Ben reiterated his earlier demand to know more. "What did you say?"

"I was coming to town and down along the river on the east side where I rode into the willows to let my horse drink, all hell was going on over across where I could make out a big old Missouri wagon and a canvas-camp. Raiders was rounding up a nice bunch of big stout mules."

Ben did not wait to hear more. He spun and raced for the door. Some patrons turned and raised their eyebrows. Jeff also left the saloon in a rush.

They met down at the liverybarn where they rigged out both animals without speaking, flung up over leather and lit up through town in a furious charge. A drunk who was crossing towards the saloon with erect and ponderous dignity, squawked when a running horse suddenly appeared from the dark and hit him glancingly with a shoulder. The drunk went backwards, somersaulted completely and landed flat out on his back. He groaned and dazedly blinked at the high heavens. Drake Haslett was hurrying across the road, had to jump to avoid the prone figure, and turned back to angrily grasp the drunk's shirt and wrench him to his feet, turn the unsteady man and propel him in the direction of the log jailhouse.

"Gawddamn you, Tom," he exclaimed, butting the drunk on down the plankwalk with a fist in the man's back. "I've told you and told you . . . And now you've taken to lying down in the middle of the road!"

"Sheriff—may the Good Lord strike me dead—I wasn't lyin' out there in the road. Some crazy bastard on a. . . ."

"The hell you wasn't lying out there. Don't you lie to me, Tom Bradley, or I'll throw the key away! Now get in there and empty your pockets into your hat, and shut up. Not a single word because I'm in a hurry. Hurry up!"

It was a warm night with clear stars and a scimitar-moon, and once horsemen got well away from town it was also a very quiet night until they veered towards the Mescal River, then the soft-lapping sound of water was audible providing anyone wanted to slow their racing horses enough to appreciate the sound.

To cover a fair distance on speeding horses never took very long. Ben and Jeff reached their camp within minutes of leaving Lincoln.

The camp itself had not been bothered, and that seemed bizarre. Not right then it didn't, but later on they commented on the singularity of a raid which passed over expensive horse-gear and mule-harness, weapons and even personal effects, to concentrate exclusively upon livestock.

In fact later on Sheriff Haslett was to re-emphasize what he had told them before. Talador's trade-mark was exactly this kind of a raid. He came in lightning-swift, made his round-up and hardly even slackened pace as he sped away as suddenly as he had arrived. Evidently his men were not allowed to halt and dismount, not even to raid a camp.

Ben and Jeff only wasted a moment or two at the canvas-camp, then punched their mounts over into a lope and headed with a little more wariness on up the riverside to the area where the mules had been serenely grazing the last time either man had seen them.

There was not a mule. Not a single one anywhere throughout the riverbank-underbrush or among the willows and cottonwoods. Jeff jumped to earth and flung his reins over a willow-branch, drew his Colt and plunged ahead into the darkness of the twisted willow-growth. He had no difficulty at all following a fresh trail of broken willows, trampled weeds and grass to the river's edge. There, he could sense roiled water and stopped to peer across.

The Mescal was not much of a river, except in a desert country where the least impressive trickle of water was considered eminently worthwhile. The Mescal had deep, narrow places but only northward where it was squeezed between mountain-flanks. Down this far southward in open country it was wider and very shallow. In some places, in fact, it was difficult for bathers to get all their lumps and bumps completely covered when they lay out flat, and here where Ben came up beside his partner in bitter silence, the raiders had had no difficulty at all in driving eighteen fine big strong mules across the river.

4

A PLACE ON THE EAST DESERT

Drake Haslett was adamant about one thing. "Don't go charging across the river and on down their back-trail, because that son of a bitch will post watchers to bushwhack you just like he did old Burns and his *vaqueros*."

"What are we supposed to do, then?" demanded Jeff. "We got a fair fortune tied up in those mules. It's taken us five years to get this special bunch together. There's not a kicking nor biting mule in that whole herd, and not a balky mule nor an old mule. Drake; that kind of livestock is worth its weight in gold!"

"I know," said the lawman. "I know exactly how you feel, but if you go busting out after Talador you'll never even see your mules again."

Ben said, "What then?"

"I'll get up a posse in town and send someone over to Fort Sheridan to. . . ."

"You said at the saloon you'd already got the army

looking for him, and you told us there was a posse of rangemen on his trail."

"Well; maybe not exactly on his trail," hedged the lawman. "They're down south of Lincoln somewhere, though, looking for him because of that other raid. The one where he cleaned out old Burns. But of course that was easterly more than southward, I think."

Ben kept staring at the lawman in the lovely warm night, until he turned to his horse and said, "Come along, Jeff," to his partner.

Sheriff Haslett was still calling to them when they splashed across the Mescal.

Ben was obdurate and as grim as death. Jeff was just as willing, but he was also just detached enough in his interest to remember all the admonitions Sheriff Haslett had put upon them.

But he only mentioned this once. That was as they were loping easily and comfortably southward upon the far side of the river from Lincoln, and Jeff said, "We better slack off a little until daylight and we can see what we're riding into."

Ben's reaction was savage. "You want to slack off—go right ahead. Drake Haslett's a nice feller but he sure-Lord's not my idea of a good lawman. He'd have us setting around town right now being warned about this mule-thievin' renegade, and we'd be a day behind no matter how we rode afterwards."

Jeff said no more, but he was wary and as watchful as it was possible to be in the darkness. He derived a little satisfaction from the fact that bushwhackers—if they were out there somewhere, waiting—would not be able to see the loping freighters any sooner, with luck, than the freighters would see them.

Two miles below town they found one of their mules. He had evidently got tired of being pushed hard, and in the night had done as many a sly mule had done over the centuries; he had pretended to be going along when in fact he had been looking for a big-enough thicket to duck into and stand with his head down until the thieves and their other charges had raced on past.

Ben said, "That's Sid. Darn mule anyway. But this is one time him hiding was in our favour."

They only paused a moment to make certain their mule was not injured, then they left Sid and struck out again. This time it was Ben who turned cautious.

"We're close," he told his partner. "Sid was still breathing hard."

They held their pace down and turned off the trail to angle more easterly. Their idea was now to try and parallel the raiders, not directly pursue them.

Time passed and the pleasant warmth began to drop down to a light chill which, later, became a more noticeable coldness in the shank of the night.

Because they knew this countryside—there were no areas of lower or central Arizona they did not know—it was possible for them to discuss the probable course of Talador and his riders.

If their purpose were indeed to get across the line with the stolen mules, then they had about three days of hard riding ahead of them, and while neither Ben nor Jeff worried about the mules being unable to take that kind of hastening, they wanted to at least be in view of their animals before the border was reached.

But it did not seem to Jeff as though Talador, if he were indeed bound for Mexico with the mules, could be as clever and wily as Drake Haslett had claimed. Talador had probably just returned from peddling that old horse-rancher's animals over the line. It would be foolish in Ben's opinion to believe another band of stolen animals could be taken down over the identical route only a few days later, and even assuming Talador would believe his enemies would not think he might try the same thing twice—and he would therefore be safe to attempt it—if he had as much sense as he was supposed to have he would certainly realize there would be cattlemen as well as army patrols down here looking for him, and in the night it would be a simple matter to accidentally encounter one, or the other—or both.

Finally, Ben drew aside heading for a little sump-spring he knew of, and when they got over there in the rank ripgut and cottonwoods, he and Jeff eased off their cinches, slipped the bridles and squatted like broncos to smoke and quietly talk and keep an eye on their resting, grazing horses.

"If that whelp is going down over the line," Ben said, "I'll eat my hat."

Jeff had evidently also come up with some deductions of his own because he answered tartly. "With army patrols down there and cattlemen somewhere behind him? Naw. At least *I* wouldn't try it, in his boots. I'd head for Verde Wells or maybe Gila. I'd go east, not south. There'll be buyers at Gila for the mules. There've always been more outlaws at Verde Wells than any other kind of folks; those mules would sell well over there, too." Jeff eyed his partner. "Question is: Which one?"

Ben was untroubled at the prospect of having to make this decision. "Come daylight we'll know," he said, and blew smoke. "But come daylight they'll be able to make us out. There's too much open country to the east."

Ben stood up, dropped his cigarette and ground it underfoot and critically looked at their saddle-stock.

No horse ever foaled could take the kind of use these animals had been taking and would have to continue to take until after daybreak, without drooping. It bothered Ben because he was a good stockman; it went against his grain to over-use or abuse animals.

Uniquely, this same compassion did not extend to humans. Especially the kind of humans he and Jeff were now seeking to find. Ben shared this distinction with most other stockmen whose feelings for animals only rarely was also sufficient to cover people.

They left the sump-spring and did not ride out of a fast walk for several miles. It was their discussed opinion that by now Talador was no longer running because he had put sufficient land between himself and the canvas-camp on the Mescal. If there were pursuit—and Talador probably did not believe there was because it would seem improbable to him that two freighters would come after him the way Ben and Jeff were doing—but if there was pursuit, from now on he would not have to flee from it as much as he would have to watch for it.

Jeff shrewdly guessed that the raiders would be waiting for daylight as much as their pursuers were, in order to find traces of rising dust. Jeff was sanguine about that because as long as he and Ben rode at a walk, they would scuff up no dust.

For that reason they broke over into a lope for a full hour, and when the first thin streak of pale grey appeared upon the far horizon to presage dawn, they dropped back down to a walk, having covered another several miles.

Ahead, invisible yet but solidly over there, were two towns. The first one, Gila, was an old Indian *pueblo* which the Mexicans had taken over a century earlier, and which subsequently the Americans had taken over. It was not as large as Lincoln, and in fact was closer actually to being a village than a town.

Beyond Gila was a larger settlement, Verde Wells, which had been notorious as an outlaw-town for many years, and periodically U.S. Marshals flanked by cavalry units rode in, and as they arrived in one end of town, the fugitives from both Mexican and U.S. law rode hastily out the other end.

Verde Wells had a law-abiding element, but it was never as bold nor assertive as the other variety of inhabitants, which was probably true in most towns.

Both Gila and Verde Wells were well-known for dealing in stolen livestock down across the border, and in fact it had been said for years that this was a two-way road; almost as many Mexican horses and cattle came north for resale, as U.S. livestock went south.

As Ben and Jeff rode towards Gila it was Ben's opinion that they should split up and enter town from opposite ends. He thought it was very possible that whether Talador knew them by sight or not, the moment Talador appeared with freight-mules to sell it would be assumed that he had raided a freighter camp, and the same day, when a pair of freighters also entered town, if Talador were still around, someone would whisper to him that Hurley and Hill must have shagged him every inch of the way.

Also, anyone who bought mules from the raider-chieftain only to suspect they were about to lose their mules to the legal owners, would be in a very bad mood towards Talador or whoever had peddled the mules in Gila.

It was reasonable to assume, then, that if Talador were still in the area, or if he were in Gila and had not yet been able to dispose of the mules, and saw two freighters entering town—he would try to kill them if for no other reason than to silence them.

Jeff accordingly split off from Ben a mile from Gila and rode southward down where the curving stageroad came up out of the south country to meander a little before it went arrow-straight for the last half mile directly into town.

Ben struck out overland for the northern environs of Gila, up where people of questionable worth had their shacks and hovels, and even a few had created Mexican adobe *jacals*. The outskirts of Gila were depressing to view. Like so many south-desert towns in Arizona, Gila eked out a bare existence by being on the north–south coachroad where all the traffic passing through, including freight and passenger and emigrant traffic, hopefully halted for a day or two and stocked up on supplies, had horses and mules shod, bought a few drinks and maybe gambled a little before striking out again.

Gila was in poor cattle country; it was over where the desert-like thin, gravelly soil supported goats and a few slab-sided, orrey-eyed, wicked-horned Mex cattle, but where worthwhile cattle could not survive.

Its greatest asset of course was its proximity to the border, as well as its somewhat insular and isolated location. There were outlaws residing quietly in Gila who had been undetected for fifteen years.

They were the latent outlaws, the ones who had been content not to return to the back-trails and the moonlight raids. When Ben entered Gila from the north, threading his way in and out among the crooked byways to reach the main thoroughfare, he saw a wizened man with a thin knife-scar on his right cheek, high up, come to the door of a tarpaper shack and stonily watch. It was Ben's guess that older man was one of the rengades which kept Gila from becoming just another ageless and timeless Mex-town of the border country.

He also wondered if that man would pass along news of the arrival in town of a stranger who had clearly been in the saddle all night. It would not take much of a stockman to make that determination from the condition of the horse under Ben.

Gila was a composite of old adobe buildings, functional and ugly, and newer wooden structures created by the Americans, which were more commodious, had higher ceilings, but which were just as ugly in a different way, and the barn where Ben swung off his horse and handed the reins to the Mexican youth who seemed to be the dayman, was an example of both adobe and wood. Evidently the barn had at one time been some kind of store or Mex *cantina,* but when the new owner had taken over he had added another length to the structure—in wood—so the effect was half bad adobe and half bad wood.

In Spanish, Ben asked the youth if they had public corrals anywhere around Gila. The boy nodded and pointed across the road. "Out back," he said in English, "over there behind the jailhouse."

Ben nodded, waited until the boy had walked away leading Ben's horse, then Ben slowly turned southward and saw a rider walking his head-hung horse up the lower stretch of thoroughfare. He did not wait, he struck out in the direction indicated by the liverybarn dayman.

When Jeff came up and saw Ben walking out behind the jailhouse, the only structure in town which had not been changed at all in well over a century, and which was recognizable by the narrow, barred windows, Jeff reined over into the yard of the liverybarn too, but when the youth came to get Jeff's horse, Jeff walked on down into the cool old gloomy interior of the barn to see that both horses were watered and grained, then cuffed and stalled and hayed. Jeff was in no hurry, not if Ben was already undertaking the investigation which had brought them here.

The morning was pleasant; sunshine, which could soften and obscure so much ugliness in the world, made Gila look almost benign, and the man with the heavy paunch who was leaning in shade up beside an old tree north of the jailhouse chewing a toothpick, considered the arrival of two strangers within moments of each other with an expression of sardonic interest. He had a dull old battered constable's badge on his shirtfront. He looked to be a person who had just finished breakfast, and in fact the building directly behind him was a café. The only one in Gila.

He rolled a cigarette, lit it, exhaled grey smoke and started walking down in the direction of the little side-road where Ben had gone. Otherwise, he seemed to be the only person up and stirring this early in Gila.

He wore a tied-down gun and run-over boots. He had a puffy face, small pale eyes that never rested, and when he walked despite his heaviness and his paunch, his stride was light.

Jeff saw him as he turned down the side-road where Ben had gone. Jeff also saw the badge and the tied-down gun. He flipped the Mexican dayman an extra two-bits and under the youth's wide and appreciative grin, Jeff winked and walked forth from the liverybarn to wait, to give that paunchy lawman plenty of time to get on his way, then Jeff sauntered out into the roadway, crossed it and also entered the little side-road.

There was not another soul in sight the full length

of Gila's main roadway. There was no one in sight down the side-road either, excepting the town constable, and ahead of him over where some gnawed and patched wooden corrals stood, Ben Hurley.

Eastward, sunlight came in brilliant shafts of golden light, flatways to the gritty soil and the sparse vegetation out there as far as a man could see.

5

A SCENT OF TROUBLE

The paunchy lawman eased up behind Ben, who was studying the old corrals, and said, "Mister; can I help you any?" and when Ben turned—and saw his partner back a hundred yards leaning in building-shadows half-hidden—he had an answer for the Gila Township constable.

"Maybe, Marshal, maybe. I'm looking for some mules."

The lawman spat out his frayed toothpick. "Mules?"

"Yeah; eighteen head of mules raided out of a canvas-camp over on the Mescal above Lincoln last night."

The lawman looked left and right. "I ain't seen no mules. You shagged the feller who stole 'em?"

"Yeah. You ever hear of an Apache named Talador?"

The lawman nodded his head without any hesitation. "Sure. That's who got your mules?"

Ben shrugged. "Maybe. I didn't see him."

"Nobody sees Talador," said the paunchy lawman.

"Unless maybe it's a Messican or another In'ian. How many mules you lose?"

"Eighteen head. Young, big sound mules, Constable."

The lawman studied Ben for a moment before saying. "I think I've seen you before. You freight around the territory, don't you? Sometimes you haul in here to Gila."

Ben nodded. "I've hauled into Gila a few times."

"Sure. And these here mules. They'll be your string for the wagon?"

"Yeah. Constable; who buys livestock in your town?"

The lawman's small eyes puckered nearly closed and his face, which was heavy and coarse, also squeezed up into an expression of either dislike or distaste. "Listen," he told Ben, "no one's got your mules around Gila. I'd know if they had. The only trader we got here in town who'd be able to handle that much of a deal would be Jess Hughes, the liveryman, and he's over to Madisonville and won't be back for another week or so. His daughter's married to the gunsmith over there and she's fixing to foal and she's old Jess's only kid, you see, so he went over to be with her."

"Any dust rise out back of town this morning?" enquired Ben, not the least bit concerned with some woman over in Madisonville who was about to give birth. "Any dust last evening before sundown?"

The lawman shook his head to both questions. "Freighter, I'm telling you, no one around here has your mules, and if some rag-head rode in and tried to peddle eighteen big young valuable mules. . . ." The lawman shook his head. "Around here, friend, an Apache couldn't sell water to thirsty folks. We got too many reasons never to trust one of 'em."

When Ben glanced over the heavy-set man's shoulder Jeff was no longer back there. Ben loosened a little and leaned to roll a smoke as he said, "Constable, if you hear of anyone buying or selling eighteen good harness mules, you let Drake Haslett know over in Lincoln." Ben lit up, looked steadily at the constable, and with no trace of malice also said, "And mister, if when I find this raider and he tells me someone from Gila slipped him a warning—I'll be back for you."

Ben turned to retrace his steps to the front roadway, but as he stepped past the paunchy lawman the constable reached a detaining hand and growled.

"Wait a minute, freighter. You don't ride into my town and make no threats to me or anyone else."

Ben jerked his arm free and whirled up close against the heavier man. His glare was icy. "That wasn't any threat, 'possum-belly, that was a goddamn promise!"

He turned and briskly walked on up to the front roadway, looked left and right without seeing his partner, saw the glass window of the café with the sign painted across it, and struck out in that direction.

Behind him the paunchy constable also came forth from that side-road. He halted to watch Ben strike out across the road on a diagonal course, then the lawman went directly over to the liverybarn.

He found the Mexican youth over there and said, "That freighter who come in a while back, the first feller, the one who entered town from the north—did he say anything to that other stranger who rode in— the feller who come from the south?"

The youth shook his head. "When the second stranger arrived the first one was already across the road. He asked me where the public corrals were, then hiked right on over there."

"But they're together," said the constable. "Didn't you get that idea?"

The youth spread his hands. "All I know, *Señor Jefe*, is that I've never seen either of them before, and they came into town at about the same time. That's all."

The constable stood thoughtfully silent for a moment before saying, "All right. Forget I said anything," he then strolled back out into the sunlight and headed over to his office at the jailhouse. There, he stood in shadows smoking a cigarette and keeping an eye upon the café.

At the liverybarn the lanky man who stepped out of the harness-room smiled at the wide-eyed Mexican youth. "The constable sure takes an interest, don't he?" he said quietly. "Can't be too careful these days, for a fact. *Amigo*; you answered his questions, now answer just one for me: Has a raider named Talador ever visited this town?"

The hostler's face paled. "Mister, I just do my work. I get paid two dollars a week to dung out the stalls and cuff the horses and mind the barn when Mister Hughes isn't around. Mister; believe me, that's what I do full-time. I don't even hear the gossip."

"What I asked, *amigo*, is whether Talador ever came to Gila?" Jeff smiled. "A simple answer is all I need. And it'll be a strict secret."

"Mister; I've heard talk of Talador over in Mextown, out back of the corrals and the jailhouse, but I don't think he's ever come here. If he has, I've never heard of it. That's gospel truth, mister."

Jeff flipped a silver cartwheel to the youth, and winked. "You forget I asked, and I'll forget that you answered."

The youth stared after lanky Jeff Hill as the older man walked away.

Across the road at the jailhouse the dayman could faintly make out the menacing face of the constable peering intently from a jailhouse window. The youth pocketed the silver cartwheel and went back to work keeping his back to the roadway. He wanted as little as possible to do with the constable.

Jeff did not go to the café. He had seen Ben head up in that direction, so he went instead to the opposite side of the roadway, to the saloon, and his entry awakened a dozing barman who was grizzled and grey and scarred. He looked to be an old soldier, perhaps an old cavalryman. As Jeff strolled over the barman beamed a big wide smile showing four gold teeth in front, and said, "What'll it be, friend?"

"Beer," replied Jeff. "And an answer to just one question."

The saloonman's shrewd eyes lingered on Jeff as he went to pump the glass full of beer. "What's the question?" he asked, skimming off surplus foam with a stiff forefinger and placing the glass on the bar.

"Has a man named Talador ever raided around here?"

The barman blinked. "You an Indian Agent?"

"No," said Jeff, hoisting the glass.

"A federal lawman, then?"

Jeff drank, set the glass aside fixed the barman with a look and said, "That's two questions I've answered for you. Now how about you answering my questions, mister?"

"Well . . . yeah, Talador's raided around here, but not since last year. But he's raided over at Lincoln. We've heard tales. . . ."

"How about Verde Wells?" asked Jeff, and the barman puckered his broad, low brow in thought, then slowly shook his head.

"Nope. Don't recall hearing of him raiding over there."

Jeff smiled, finished his beer, tossed down a coin and strolled back outside, arriving there just in time to see the paunchy lawman duck back inside his jailhouse, while up the road on the opposite side, Ben was leaving the café.

Jeff waited until he knew Ben had seen him in front of the saloon, then he also turned and walked southward towards the lower end of town.

By this time Gila's stores were beginning to seem busy and there were people in the roadway, not many but enough so that when Ben and Jeff converged upon the liverybarn they were not especially conspicuous. In fact, when they walked in down there a short, thick, dark man driving a fine, fringed-top surrey was just alighting for the Mexican youth to take over and lead his rig down the runway. The squatty man nodded and strode past Ben and Jeff on his way up through town.

Otherwise, though, there did not appear to have been much business at the barn since Hurley and Hill had ridden in more than an hour earlier, and now, as the dayman was unbuckling harness to take the horse from between the surrey's shafts, Jeff said he and his partner would get their own animals, which the youth smiled about. He was already favourable towards Jeff.

Later, when the youth had the fine-harness animal stalled and fed, and when the men from Lincoln were ready to lead their horses out front before mounting, the Mexican walked up to Jeff and quietly said, "Mister; how good are you at keeping something to yourself?"

Jeff grinned. "Been doing it all my life without a bit of trouble."

"You know which man is our town constable here in Gila?" the youth asked, and when Jeff nodded the youth then said, in a lowered tone of voice, "He come in here and asked about you and the other feller. That man over there." The youth looked out back, then up front towards the empty yard and roadway beyond. "Mister, there's been talk about our constable for a long while. I don't know whether any of it's true or not, but there's been talk."

"What kind of talk?" Jeff asked. "Like maybe he might not be the most honest feller in town?"

"Yes. That kind of talk."

Jeff fished in a pocket, brought forth half a cartwheel and shoved it into the lad's hand. "Don't worry; no one will ever hear it from me that we talked." He winked and turned to lead his horse out front.

He said nothing until he and Ben were heading eastward beyond Gila on the Verde Wells road, then he mentioned something else which was on his mind first, before he mentioned the Gila lawman.

"Saloon-keeper back there told me Talador raids the Lincoln countryside."

"You knew that," said Ben Hurley.

"He also told me Talador raided around Gila last year."

Ben turned and eyed his partner. "What are you leading up to?"

"He hasn't raided over around Verde Wells."

"Well; maybe his territory don't stretch that far, Jeff."

"And maybe," stated Jeff, "it does. If he's raided as far from Gila as Lincoln, it's not as far over to Verde Wells from Gila, as it is to Lincoln from Gila."

Ben screwed up his face. "What the hell does that mean?"

"I got a notion the reason he don't raid over around Verde Wells is because that's one place he don't want a bad reputation . . . There are a lot of fugitives over there. Verde Wells's had that reputation ever since I can recall. It's an outlaw-town. If Talador's got contacts over there he could peddle a lot of good stolen livestock and never even have to go down into Mexico. If he is doing that. . . ."

"He wouldn't want to jeopardize anything," concluded Ben Hurley, and twisted in his saddle to look back across the open, empty, sun-washed land between where they were riding and the village they had recently ridden from.

"And there's something else," stated Jeff. "That lawman in Gila was asking questions about us."

Ben straightened forward. "Yeah; I guessed as much. The feller in the café told me to mind that *hombre*, that he's not only real nosy and treacherous, but he's also a little shy of being a paragon of virtue."

"A what?"

"Darned if I know. That's what the caféman called him and I think it means he's an underhanded subbitch." Ben rolled a smoke and lit it as he also said, "We came over here lookin' for trouble didn't we?"

"We came over here lookin' for *mules*," stated Jeff, making a firm correction, but his partner looked mildly disgusted about that.

"We're going to have one before we get the other," he said, "and I'll bet you a new hat on that!" Then he smiled and stood in the stirrups again, twisted to look back, and made a little clucking sound of disapproval as he eased forward again in the saddle.

"Folks in Gila don't much like their lawman, I'd say, and right about now I'm beginning to feel a little that way, myself. Look back and keep looking."

Ben obeyed, he rode ahead with his body sideways in the saddle. At first he noticed nothing in particular, but as they continued to cross more or less open country he finally detected movement, and after a long while he located the man riding the dark horse who was clearly doing his best to keep the freighters in sight while simultaneously avoiding detection, himself. But from time to time he could not avoid crossing open places, and it was while he was doing this, swiftly and stealthily, that Ben had seen him and Jeff now also saw him.

Jeff straightened up and scratched his head, dropped the hat back down while studying the onward countryside, and arrived at a conclusion. "He's not trying to keep us in sight as much as he's tryin' to get around us, around past us on the same course."

Ben had already guessed this, and a little more. "To get ahead of us, Jeff, on the same trail as we're ridin' means he wants to get ahead of us and reach Verde Wells before we do. Now I wonder why he'd want to do that—except to tell someone up ahead that we're coming, and that damned well could mean someone settin' up an ambush for us."

Jeff looked back again, then frowned as he swung forward and began to study the forward flow of countryside. "I got a confession to make," he told his partner, while looking ahead and on both sides. "Try as I have, I just plain never liked cow-town constables. I realize there are decent ones, and I know a man hadn't ought to say he don't like all one kind of folks, but I'm here to tell you I just never liked cow-town lawmen. And this one—you see that big thicket up ahead about a mile and a half, to the east a little?"

Ben knew which thicket his partner was referring to so he nodded his head.

"Well; you ride on in there with me, and you keep right on ridin' out the far side, and sing or whistle or something, and lead my horse so's he'll see the tracks of us both—and I'm going to step into the underbrush and when he goes by I'm going to jump him like I was an Apache."

Ben said, "How do you know it's the constable?"

"If it isn't, someone's going to learn never to ride through a big thicket again, isn't he?"

Ben chuckled. "You're plain mean," he told his partner. "Ornery and mean." Then he puckered up to whistle as he rode along.

6

THE TRIO

The thicket ran roughly parallel to the course they had been following so they had to angle slightly north-ward to reach it and they had to accomplish this in as casual a manner as possible.

But they had more than a mile to gradually change their route that much, so it was entirely possible and most important, it did not look as though they were consciously heading into the thicket.

Like many growths of underbrush in an arid, gritty territory of poor soil this thicket prospered because it had originally taken root in one of the rare areas where actual underground nourishment was unsus-pectingly adequate.

It covered about ten acres of land and was, aside from being ideal for ambushes, the private world of desert wrens, gila monsters, rattlesnakes, crawling things by the hundreds, and upon occasion and in season, whelping coyotes and little swift-foxes.

But none of those thicket inhabitants were willing to dispute the passage of a pair of horsemen, particularly since horsemen had come through here before and had never tarried. The wild creatures simply pulled back as stealthily as possible and prepared themselves to wait until the horsemen had gone by.

As far as Jeff Hill was personally concerned anything residing in the thorny thicket was entirely welcome to it. He did not even consider lingering in there one moment longer than he had to, and in fact when he handed Ben his reins and slid to the ground his entire concern with doing something swiftly and getting back out of there took total precedent.

Ben worked his way back and forth through the thicket, utilizing a number of the runways in there, his primary effort having to do with locating runways which were wide enough to accommodate a rider leading a second horse, and there were none too many of that kind of trail.

He whistled as he rode, and occasionally affected a loud laugh, the effect being to successfully dupe anyone close enough or interested enough.

His partner ducked back into the thicket and waited, scarcely breathing. The tracks were plain, the visibility for the following horseman was very limited once he entered the thicket, and once Jeff became stationary, the wrens began their busy chirping again. All he needed now was for the rider to come walking along and he remained half-hidden and alert, waiting.

It seemed a lifetime before he heard rein-chains, or the belated shuffle of shod hooves across gravelly soil. Evidently the rider was following tracks now, since it was improbable that he could see beyond the first rank of the thicket.

He had evidently delayed his entrance into the thicket on purpose in order to remove all chance of being discovered by the horsemen up ahead. Normally he would have been quite safe from discovery, particularly in a thicket, but this time his urge to get ahead of Ben and Jeff had already permitted them to realize he was back there.

His horse lifted its head as though catching a scent. Jeff could make out the horse when he did this but he still could not see the man very well. Not well enough, at any rate. But the man seemed oblivious to his horse's suspicion and urged the animal on through.

Jeff finally saw the man. It was the constable from Gila! Apparently all that the Mexican youth at the liverybarn had hinted at, back in Gila, was true, with much more which had been left unsaid, also being true.

Jeff pulled back a little and crouched. He was standing uncomfortably within the thorny first row of growth alongside the trail Ben had taken and which the constable was now also taking.

The wrens became silent again. Nothing moved anywhere throughout the thicket as a fresh man-scent fanned out under the hot sun.

The lawman's mount continued to evince interest in a scent and the constable just as consistently ignored the horse, or perhaps was one of those people who simply rode horses, who did not appreciate them nor understand them.

Finally, the horse changed leads and turned his head in Jeff's direction. This time the rider was sufficiently annoyed to swear at the animal. He was doing this when Jeff launched himself upwards and dead ahead. The horse might have reacted speedily enough to save the constable, by shying sideways, but he was concentrating on the reaction of his rider to his having changed leads and did not recover sufficiently to shy until Jeff had collided with the man on the horse's back, and they were both tumbling. Then the horse shied, and by then the saddle was empty.

For Jeff the horse was unimportant once he'd decided to attack. In fact when the animal shied, Jeff and the lawman were already on their way to the ground so the horse moving clear simply facilitated their fall, and because Jeff had known exactly what he was doing and the completely astonished constable was too stunned to know anything, it was possible for Jeff to ride the lawman to the ground with the constable below and with Jeff on top.

The ground did not knock the breath out of the lawman but it added to his stunned amazement when it hit him solidly in the back, and yet the man's co-ordination was excellent; he was reaching for his Colt seconds after striking the ground and Jeff may have been fortunate that they had come down so hard, because the lawman's holstered sixgun had skittered ten feet away when they struck, and the man's hand arrived at an empty holster. He had been fast. Probably faster than Jeff would have been, and that was what allowed Jeff to remain alive and to avoid having to make a test of speed.

It also did something else. It removed the lawman's right hand and arm from the vicinity of his face, so when Jeff grabbed shirtcloth and wrenched the lawman's head and shoulders off the ground, then swung and connected, the lawman turned loose all over. What the fall to the ground had not done Jeff Hill's bony right fist had done.

He eased the unconscious man down, arose from astraddle him and stepped over where that sixgun had skittered. Then he gave the call of a mourning dove.

Moments later when Ben appeared on foot, hand on his holster, Jeff had unloaded the constable's Colt and had returned it to the lawman's holster. He started to dust himself off as Ben walked into the clearing, stepped past Jeff after one appraising look, and got a closer view of the unconscious man. Ben clucked.

"You may be right," he conceded. "Cow-town lawmen may not be folks a body'd ought to admire." Ben turned. "You all right?"

Jeff grinned. "Yeah. Tore my shirt a little in the damned thicket, otherwise I'm fine."

Ben leaned and roughly rolled the lawman up on to his side, pulled a fat wallet from the unconscious man's rear pocket, thumbed through it and removed a greenback which he handed his partner, then he returned the wallet and said, "For a new shirt."

Jeff pocketed the money and a moment later the lawman groaned and stretched one arm to run his hand along the gritty ground as though making certain where he was. Ben and Jeff stood aside watching. Evidently the constable had a tough skull because Jeff had struck him with a lot of power. Other men would have been "out" for a lot longer.

The lawman flopped on to his back, blinked up at the pair of unsmiling men, and after a moment of staring he heaved with both arms to prop himself, and continued to stare in that position for another short while before finally raising up into a sitting position.

He felt his jaw. It was not discoloured yet but the swelling was shaping up. By the time the swelling and the discoloration were fully developed the constable from Gila was going to look as though his head were larger on one side than upon the other side.

Jeff leaned to extend a hand. "Get up," he ordered, and gripped the extended fist to help. When the lawman was on his feet, not too steadily, Jeff said, "Mister, what's your name?"

The lawman felt his jaw very gingerly before replying. "Hank Armstrong."

"Hank, how come you were trying to get around us and beat us over to Verde Wells?"

Armstrong raised sultry eyes. "Who said I was trying to get around you?"

"I said it," replied Jeff, and balanced forward just the slightest bit.

Constable Armstrong surmised Jeff's purpose in leaning towards him a little and acted as though he might turn away and step back before he was struck again. "I had business over there," he said, watching Jeff closely. "Nothing wrong with a man transacting a little business, that I know of."

Ben looked dour when he said, "We don't have all day. Let's get the son of a bitch on his horse and take him along."

They did that. They caught Armstrong's mount and rode on through the thicket with him and out the far side into open country again none of them with a word to say until they were well away from the thicket and Ben turned to gesture for Armstrong to ride up between Ben and Jeff.

"Where did you figure to contact Talador?" Ben asked.

The constable scowled. "What the hell kind of question is that?" he growled. "I've never laid eyes on that lousy renegade in my life."

Ben pondered, then tried another approach. "Who were you going to warn about us coming over there?"

Armstrong looked more disgusted than upset now. "Who says I care what you two are up to? Mister, I've never seen Talador nor your lousy mules."

Ben tried another tack, this one based upon his

knowledge of what constituted a lie, and a liar, in cattle country—and presumably elsewhere. He said, "Hank, you're not going to reach Verde Wells, and you got my word on it." Then he also said, "All right; you never saw Talador and you've never seen our mules. As for who says you were riding to Verde Wells to warn someone—I say it. You care to call me a liar?"

Armstrong's coarse features settled into a stubborn and embittered expression. He rode along looking at Ben Hurley without opening his mouth.

He might have been able to find some sign of compassion in the other freighter's face, but there was not a shred nor a hint of it in Ben Hurley's expression. Of the two freighters, clearly the shorter man was the least likely to be tolerant or lenient. When he said Hank Armstrong was not going to reach Verde Wells, he was not bluffing.

Armstrong said, "I'm not calling anyone a liar, mister."

Ben nodded encouragingly. "That's a fair start. It'll keep you alive for another hundred yards." Ben looked ahead for a landmark. "Until we reach that red shale-stone on ahead."

Armstrong looked, saw the shale-stone, fished forth a plug of chewing tobacco from a shirt-pocket, gnawed off a corner, replaced the plug and turned aside to expectorate, then he glared accusingly at Jeff, as though this entire thing were his fault, and said, "You figure I'm going to ride into Verde Wells with you fellers? That town has two-thirds of its menfolk on someone's wanted list somewhere, and it'll be bad enough me just wearing my badge, but showing up over there with. . . ."

"We can figure all that out," exclaimed Ben, cutting across the bitter flow of words. "Mister, you're almost up to the shale-rock."

But Armstrong did not relent. "I'll tell you this much. You kill me and there'll be an investigation. There always is."

"Who," growled Ben Hurley. "Who, Hank? Who were you riding over yonder to warn about us coming?"

They were within thirty yards of the red shale. Jeff leaned a little in his saddle, the way men do when they draw a sixgun, but Jeff's right side was beyond the visibility of Hank Armstrong. Then Jeff settled back and stoically rode along.

They rode ten yards, then five yards. Suddenly Hank Armstrong bit down hard on his cud and went for his sixgun.

Jeff twisted in the saddle, Colt in his lap. On the other side Ben drew rein and sat with both hands atop the saddlehorn coldly eyeing the lawman with the gun in his fist. Armstrong said, "I know your partner's got me covered from in back, mister, but if he pulls a trigger you die along with me."

Ben shook his head. "Hank, up-end that silly gun and look into the cylinder. It's not loaded."

For a moment the constable stared in disbelief, then his expression slowly changed as he analysed the expression on Ben Hurley's face, and he tilted up his Colt, tilted it up a little more and looked down.

With a wild curse he flung the gun from him out into the gravelly desert. Behind him Jeff cocked his gun. The sound was unmistakable even when there was no gun in sight.

"Lem Steele," Armstrong spat out. "I was on my way to tell Lem Steele over in Verde Wells you fellers was on your way. I should have figured some way to keep you back there at Gila, but that never crossed my mind until I was already in the saddle."

Ben brushed that aside to ask who Lem Steele was, and the lawman frowned anew. "You must not have been to Verde Wells lately," he growled. "Lem's the law over there . . . He's fast and he's suspicious, and even now that you boys know about him it's not going to do you a hell of a lot of good. He's got them two-thirds I told you about square behind him."

"Does he by any chance buy mules?" Ben asked mildly, and got another of those bitter, fierce replies.

"He buys anything!"

"From Talador?"

"From anyone!"

Ben sighed, they were abreast of the red shale. He looked around the angry lawman to Jeff and hitched his shoulders up and down. "Can't kill him now," he said, "might as well put up the gun." Then Ben turned back to Hank Armstrong with another question.

"What's your connection with Lem Steele?"

"He's got marshals and constables in every town around who get paid for information." Armstrong looked stonily ahead, down between his horse's ears and out across the empty land. "For something like I was going to be able to tell him, he'd pay right well. You know why?"

"Yeah," Ben dryly replied. "I can guess. Because the son of a bitch's got our mules."

"If he don't have them now, mister, he will have them when Talador figures it's safe to slip down and peddle them to him. Or else Talador's already sold them to Lem and they're cached in one of the back-country canyons."

Jeff said, "That answers one thing that's been bothering me. When Talador hit that old horse-rancher named Burns, and Drake said he'd shag those stolen horses down over the line into Mexico—how the hell did he ever get down there, peddle the horses and get back up to Lincoln to raid us within twenty-four hours? . . . He didn't. He delivered the horses over here, then turned back, and hell, that's not even a full one-day ride."

Ben and their prisoner both listened. The prisoner had no comment to offer and Ben simply said, "Dust it on ahead for a mile or two, will you? And sort of look around. I'm beginning to get an uneasy feeling about this country over here."

7

THE FOOTHILLS

The distance between Gila and Verde Wells was not great. If horsemen went by the road they could make very good time crossing from one town to the other. Even when they went overland and deliberately avoided the town the way Ben and Jeff had done, it was not much of a ride.

They had the rooftops and some of the more outlying corrals in sight before the sun could slant away and start to change colour very much.

Jeff had been to Verde Wells several times over the past few years but Ben had not stepped foot in the town in something like seven years, and during that period of a time many changes usually took place in normal communities let alone the kind of community Verde Wells had become over the past quarter century.

Neither of them, though, had ever heard of a man named Lem Steele, and although Jeff raked his mind to try and remember after Armstrong told them Lem Steele had been over there as lawman even during those more recent years when Jeff had passed through, it still did not mean anything to Jeff. Probably because the few times he'd been to Verde Wells in the past few years he'd had no reason to be interested in who the lawman was.

Only when Hank Armstrong begged to be set free and promised on everything most people held inviolate not to enter the place, and in fact to return to Gila and never mention stolen mules or even freighters, did Ben offer a glimmer of his strategy by saying, "Hank; we needed an ace-in-the-hole. You're kind of a gutty one, and ugly, and treacherous, and worthless, and probably illegitimate in the bargain, but you're what we got so you're what we'll use."

"Use how?" asked the lawman.

Ben offered no explanation at all. He simply said, "When Talador delivers stolen livestock over here— where does he corral 'em?"

Armstrong attempted to hedge. He professed to know nothing beyond the fact that he kept Lem Steele warned about possible danger from the direction of Gila.

Ben turned a slow look of menace upon the constable. Armstrong already had a latent mistrust, even a candid fear, of Ben Hurley, and it was one of the disadvantages of this kind of personal dread that it fed upon itself. The longer Hank Armstrong rode beside Ben Hurley the more convinced he was that Ben would kill him without a second thought.

It was this growing fear that made him finally say, "There's corrals all around, over here. They even got 'em in some of the foothill canyons to the north so's rustlers bringin' in livestock don't have to come all the way out on to the Kiowa Plains—which is what this country over here is called—all they got to do is send a rider ahead to let Lem know, then corral their animals in the hills somewhere and set down to wait until Lem rides out . . . Or sometimes he even drives out in his buggy to transact business. He's got a fine enterprise, Lem has."

In a complaining tone of voice Ben said, "For some darned reason, Hank, you just can't plain answer a question, you got to darn near give a history along with it. What I want to know is where Talador will most likely deliver our eighteen head of mules."

Armstrong reddened. After a few yards of riding he lifted an arm. "I'd guess up yonder along the foothills where the mountains sort of slope down and make a green belt—a buffer, they call it—between the desert and the mountains. I'd say Talador'll have your mules corralled up there by today some time." Armstrong dropped his arm and rode along squinting northward. In a drawling tone as though he were speaking to himself or were perhaps musing aloud for no one's particular attention, he also said, "There's a dozen good trails comin' out of them mountains. There's a hundred ways a few raiders drivin' livestock can keep out of sight until they're almost to the gates of some corralled-off canyon. My guess would be that Talador would know 'em all."

He spat out his cud of chewing tobacco, straightened in the saddle and groaned as the sight of Verde Wells appeared more distinct, now that they were still closer to it.

"You're going to get us all killed," he told Ben, looking ahead. "I told you—Verde Wells is an outlaw town. You think two freighters can just ride in and collect their mules and ride out? I wouldn't care except I'm along with you."

Ben studied the onward town. They were still a fair

distance to the west of Verde Wells when he finally made a slight correction with his reins and as his two companions also made the same slight alteration in the way they were riding Jeff smiled for no particular reason that Armstrong could imagine, except that the taller of his captors smiled more readily than the other one did.

They did not enter the town. They rode completely around it from a distance of about a mile out and twice Jeff loped closer and both times he returned to shake his head without saying a word. Armstrong eventually figured out what they were doing, but by this time Ben jutted his jaw towards the distant foothills and they changed their course once more.

Armstrong said, "He couldn't have got your mules down to town this fast. Not if they was only stole night before last from up the river above Lincoln."

Neither Ben nor Jeff commented, they were now making a steady study of the northward mountains, and down this side of them, the broken run of tawny foothills.

There was one obvious disadvantage to what they were now doing. All the territory northward of Verde Wells all the way to the foothills, had been cut over or burnt off; there was no vegetation any higher than sage, so riders would be plainly visible.

That did not necessarily have to imply direct peril because although any wary raiders up in the hills would certainly be watching, unless they knew who the men were on their way towards them, they would not have much to worry about, and if they *did* know, for example, that Constable Armstrong from Gila was one of Lem Steele's men, they wouldn't worry very much about the other two men.

Still, Ben told Jeff they would probably be under

surveillance the last couple of miles, and that evoked another groan from Hank Armstrong who said, "You're crazy. If Talador's up there. . . ."

"Yeah—if he's up there?"

"He'll kill all three of us."

"Does he know you?" asked Jeff, and when Hank shook his head Jeff said, "Take that damned badge off your shirt and put it in a pocket."

The constable obeyed but he did not see this as much of a change. "We're still three strangers in those darned foothills," he explained. "And Talador's not the only one likely to be up there. Suppose he got here early with your darned mules and sent down his messenger, and suppose Lem is up there right now hagglin' over a price."

Ben pretended indifference. "All right—suppose all those things, and the moon is made of cheese—what of it?"

Armstrong peered at Ben with an expression of absolute incredulity. "What do you mean—what of it? For Chris'sake Lem knows me and he knows I'm not supposed to be snoopin' around in his foothills. He's been making that plain to folks for years. And you two—total strangers—all I got to say is that you don't know Lem Steele or you wouldn't be doin' this. I'll tell you plain out that you're going to get yourselves killed sure as I'm setting here between the pair of you. I've yet to see the blasted mule I'd run that risk for."

"Then you've never seen our mules," responded Jeff, gazing ahead. "There's some dust to the west a mile. See it, Ben?"

"Yeah; looks as though it's comin' down from the trees—northward and maybe a little westerly . . . Talador?"

Jeff pursed his lips and did some careful figuring in his head. He arrived at the conclusion that it could indeed be the raiders with the mules. "If they went north up into the hills instead of southward like we figured," he told Ben, "it would take them just about this long to get over to Verde Wells."

Ben was not quite convinced yet. "If they drove hard all night after they crossed the river they should have been down here early this morning."

"With half the mules," stated Jeff. "You know darned well no one could drive our mules through a forest, through a bunch of hills and canyons and get down here this morning with more than three or four of them."

Hank Armstrong listened, kept his face curled into a bleak frown, and did not take his eyes off the little spindrift of brown dust as it seemed to be coming down through the trees towards the lower and less wooded foothills. "If that's Talador," he finally said, "then he'll be sending a rider on down to let Lem know he's arriving. And in case you boys didn't know it, Talador rides with six other men, he don't make no raids by himself. Where does that leave us—three of us, and me with no gun—and him with six men and plenty of guns? I told you—you're going to get us killed . . . Even if Lem ain't up there yet and comes later—we're going to be between Lem Steele and Talador."

Armstrong visibly shuddered then rolled up his eyes.

Ben ignored him. So did Jeff. They were waiting to see if it would be possible to determine what was making that dust.

Armstrong was more interested in other things; he kept looking back over first one shoulder then the other shoulder. Clearly, he could imagine no situation more hazardous than the one he was now in, and after a while when he seemed positive that from one direction or the other he and his companions had been seen, he said, "Listen; what will it take for you fellers to just let me bow out of this?"

Jeff smiled. "We'd miss your company," he said. "And it may come down to us needing someone to stand in front if shooting starts."

Armstrong did not appreciate the humour nor the teasing. He had already decided that his captors were madmen. He could not conceive of anyone in his right mind going up against either Talador or Lem Steele, and certainly not two men by themselves.

"I can dig up a little cash," he told Ben, turning his appeals in this fresh direction after getting such little satisfaction from Jeff.

Ben was a practical man. "How would we ever collect? You think we'd ought to just let you ride away from here, now, and on our way back stop in Gila for the money? Constable, you don't believe we're ever coming back."

Armstrong seemed to give it up. He grimaced, peered back over a shoulder, peered up ahead where that dust had been and where it seemed now to have dissipated throughout the treetops, then he said, "I need a weapon," and Ben agreed with him. "You sure are likely to," but Ben made no effort to do anything about supplying the lawman's deficiency even though both he and Jeff had Colts as well as Winchesters.

Armstrong chewed and spat and looked around, looked back again and finally seemed convinced his only hope for survival lay in co-operating with his captors at least until something happened which might correct his situation. He spat and ran a soiled sleeve across his lips, hitched at the britches under his paunch and pointed to a slot through the nearby foothills.

"There's a corralled-off place up yonder," he growled.

Jeff cocked a sceptical eye. "I thought you told us all you knew about Steele's business was to warn him; that you didn't know anything else, and already you've explained how he takes delivery up in here of livestock stolen over around Lincoln."

Armstrong shifted his cud and speared Jeff with an unfriendly glare. "I lied a little. I've been up here a time or two, but I've never taken part in no raids or anything like that. I've rode these foothills a few times for Lem, just to make certain there wasn't no squatters nor campers nor other folks up here." He pointed to that same slot again. "If you don't turn off to the east you're goin' to ride right on up into someone's guard. That's where the fellers with that drive was heading. It's the only decent fenced-off place for a mile in either direction." He put his hands atop the horn, chewed, squinted his eyes nearly closed and shook his head. "They've seen us by now anyway. If they got spyglasses, they'll have recognized me even if they don't know you fellers."

Jeff said, "Talador—with a spyglass?"

Hank looked annoyed. "What do you figure—he's one of them old-time rag-heads with moccasins and a breech-clout and feathers and that kind of junk? Mister, nowadays they got better guns'n we got, faster horses, and spyglasses!"

Ben reined easterly around the thick flank of a heavy low hill. He had seen no one. In fact he had not even seen any dust for more than an hour now. "I feel 'em," he told Jeff, and got a glare from Hank Armstrong, but the constable said nothing.

Jeff was more sanguine. "Be better if you could smell 'em—the mules I mean." Jeff studied each skyline as they came close to it. This was not his first scout as a distressed freighter nor did he especially want it to be his last. He had in fact been through a number of brushes with raiders, usually with Mexicans but a few times also with Indians, although he had never been able to satisfactorily say he had met Apaches. There were also Comanches who frequently raided over this far from Texas. In fact he had seen the results of Comanche war parties attacking Apache villages, and he had heard from oldtimers around the lower desert territories that at one time this had been Comanche country. They had pulled out not as a result of pressure from the Apaches, but because the lower desert was beginning to fill up with cowmen and townsmen. They had returned to Texas, although now and then a captive or a corpse was brought in from a skirmish on the Arizona low-desert and he would not be an Apache nor a Mexican, he would be a Comanche.

But to Jeff, and Ben, and presumably their prisoner, along with most other residents of lower and central Arizona Territory, an Indian was an Indian regardless of tribal affiliation or clan, and right now Jeff's interest was in trying to detect one before one detected him. At least before one got him in his gunsights.

Hank Armstrong had more than that singular worry. He seemed to be much more afraid of being caught up in this foothill country by Lem Steele and when Ben pressed him for an explanation he said, "He don't like anyone up here. He's let that be pretty widely known. Me especially; not that he's got anything against me—he don't have—but he's told me a dozen times he don't want anyone up in here unless he sends 'em."

Ben was critical. "What's so bad about you being up here? If you know he receives stolen livestock up here, and other fellers who work for him also know it —what's so bad about you fellers being up here?"

Armstrong growled his retort. "Mister, you don't know Lem Steele. If he says he don't want folks up here—that's the damned law as far as he's concerned. And I've already told you that once."

Ben dropped the subject. It still bothered him a little but it was not the most critical thing at this juncture in his search for stolen mules. Staying alive was, and also finding the mules, and maybe, with some luck and a lot of shrewdness, retrieving the mules.

8

A MEETING

Hank Armstrong showed them where to hide the horses and how to sneak around a hillock until they were gazing down the long, walled canyon which was gated-off at the lower end. It was what the Mexicans called a 'funnel' canyon, meaning it was easy to enter and very difficult to depart from unless one went back and departed by the same route they had used to enter it.

Some cowmen called them 'box' canyons, but whatever the designation the effect was the same; perhaps men could scale the high walls—but that was problematical too—but no four-legged critter could, so all that was required was to gate-off the lower entrance, and this had been done very well. Ben and Jeff even discussed the way that corral-off place had been set up—with mighty cedar posts and peeled fir-log stringers. Maybe, as Jeff suggested, whoever had made that fence and gate had felt justified in spending more time and perspiration down at the narrow end of the canyon, because they did not have to spend any time else-where in this particular site, building fence.

Maybe there was another reason for those mighty posts and impervious log stringers. All the livestock which was corralled back up in here was not gentle.

Ben's concern was with the fact that right now the canyon was empty, and there was no sign of anyone around. He swivelled to look elsewhere. Armstrong was lying beside him and raised his head to say, "We got here first. I figured it could happen like that." Then he also said, "Listen, fellers; there might be time to scout southward and find a cow outfit that'd help you catch Talador and his horse-thieves."

Ben and Jeff put sulphurous looks upon Hank Armstrong. The constable wilted back down into a prone position and gazed below into the empty canyon as he said, "Well; what's wrong with a body trying to figure ways not to have to die today? We get caught up here by Steele or that darned rag-head, and. . . ."

"You've made that point ten times now," Ben growled at Armstrong. He did not forbid the constable to repeat it, but the silence was inference enough. All three of them flattened atop the warm stone and peered downward.

There was sign that the canyon had been used recently. Perhaps within the last four or five days, according to Jeff's surmise. Ben shrugged that off and rolled to look up along the forested upper slope. He expected to see more dust but there was none, and that bothered him until Armstrong explained that beyond the trees and for perhaps a hundred and fifty yards back in there, a seepage-spring fed about sixty or seventy acres all along the sidehill. Animals walking through there could not make dust if they wanted to.

Ben squinted rearward as he said, "Then they could be coming down out of there any time now."

Hank nodded. "That's why I been wanting to get off this darned rock-flat up here. They'll see us. And if they're along the seepage-sidehill that'd be about where I'd expect Talador to cut his messenger loose and send him on ahead."

Ben gestured for Hank to lead the way back where they had left the horses, and as Hank obliged he utilized every bit of cover so that they would not be seen. He was going to be a nervous wreck if this kept up very long.

Jeff went to scout elsewhere, to the west for a while, and also easterly, then just before returning to the others, he slithered up a hill and lay belly-down studying the southward countryside. He did not see a rider or even any indication that there might be riders, so he went over and joined Ben and Hank Armstrong with this information. The other two men were sitting relaxed and smoking. Normally, Armstrong chewed tobacco, but like most chewers he would also smoke from time to time. Now, he continued to look very unhappy but it seemed to Jeff Hill that Armstrong was beginning to think in terms of helping his captors to survive in order to assure that he might also do the same.

He had drawn a map in the dust with a small stick and was still explaining to Ben Hurley how the landforms were spaced and positioned when Jeff arrived, and moments later it was Hank Armstrong who walked out a few yards and stood, paunch and all, studying the north-westerly final fringe of forested slope. He came back with a grunt and a gesture. "Mules or I'm a Dutchman's uncle."

All three of them went back over there, and Armstrong was correct. The animals were a good distance away and they were backgrounded by dark treestands, but an experienced person did not have to see the ears or the long faces because mules did not travel the way horses did.

Jeff said, "That's going to be one surprised son of a bitch," and Armstrong turned a sweat-shiny face to contradict that. "He ain't going to be as surprised as you fellers are if you attempt to steal back your animals. Talador's everything folks been saying, and a hell of a lot more. Gents, you don't stand a chance. Not a single lousy chance. That's the gospel-truth."

"The trouble with you," stated Jeff, looking up where those small very distant shapes were finally fully down out of the trees, "is that someone's got you so darned buffaloed you can't conceive of anyone but Talador and Steele ever winning."

Hank shot back a waspish answer to that. "Yeah? And I suppose you figure you boys are going to get those mules back and get away from here alive, just because you happened to beat the rag-heads down here. Well, let me tell you. . . ."

"Some other time," growled Ben, and Armstrong instantly became silent. He had a very healthy respect —and fear—of Ben Hurley.

Ben had developed an antagonism towards Armstrong which superseded his earlier detached feeling of scorn. For one thing, every time Ben or his partner said anything, Armstrong found fault with it. For another thing, Ben was beginning to formulate an idea of what they should do. He took Jeff aside and said, "If we could nail the messenger from Talador we could keep Steele down at Verde Wells from knowing the mules were up here. At least for a while, and if we could get a couple of hours' start, I think we might be able to make it. What do you think?"

Jeff shrugged. "I'll see if I can catch the messenger." He stared at his partner. "If I can't rope him off his horse or ambush him on the ground . . ." He and Ben looked directly at one another, then Jeff turned to go over and lift the Winchester from his saddleboot. He also took the lariat.

He left on foot and Hank Armstrong craned around with an uneasy look, to watch. He could not keep track of Jeff for long, though, because of the nature of the somewhat up-ended countryside.

For Jeff, there were several advantages. Once he got back in the vicinity of the box-canyon, got over upon the west side of it up through some stands of stone and scrub-brush which rose no more than eighteen inches off the ground, he had an excellent view of those oncoming animals, trudging along as though they were tired, or else were not being pushed too hard.

He could make out horsemen, finally, but did not get a good count of them because not only were they constantly moving, but the animals they were driving were also shifting back and forth as they hiked along, too.

Jeff wondered when Talador would detach that messenger. For Jeff's purpose if he cut the man loose before he reached the canyon it would be better.

Eventually he could count them. There were seven drovers. They set the driven animals to an old trail and from that point on actually would make out much better if they did not haze them; usually, driven animals, in strange or familiar country, would follow a marked trail if they were put upon it.

Then, from his hiding-place like a rag-head in

among the tawny rocks, Jeff saw several of those rustlers come together. Moments later one of them pulled clear of the others.

Jeff looked carefully southward to select the most plausible route for a horseman to take through the rocks, and when he was satisfied on that score he pulled back and started southward, but slowly; he had to now make certain this would be the route that rider would take, even though there actually were no other real alternatives.

A lot was riding on his success. In fact, without his partner being able to know about it, over here through the rocks above and on the west side of the box-canyon, was where all Jeff and Ben had endured since riding out of Lincoln would culminate one way or another. If Jeff failed, then the best he and Ben could hope for was to escape before Talador and perhaps his cohorts from Verde Wells overtook and killed them both.

With that kind of an incentive, Jeff went back and forth through the low spires until he got to the westernmost extremity of them and could look down where the trail went, in and out following the route of least resistance.

The other renegades had to turn easterly and cross that flat-rock ridge where Jeff and Ben and their captive had been lying while studying the box-canyon earlier. Once they got down upon the far or southerly side of that ridge they would be within the initial walls of the canyon itself, and from that point on they would not even need drivers, since all they could do, if they didn't whirl and cut back, was continue right on up into the canyon.

Jeff had a fine chance to verify the identity of those driven animals after Talador had detached his rider towards Verde Wells, and set his other riders to easing the stolen stock up the slope towards the flat-rock rim. The sun brightly shone and the clear air made things a mile distant look no more than several hundred feet away.

He could in fact even count the animals as they strung out up the trail. Seventeen big young mules! They did not seem particularly gaunted-up although to someone as experienced as Jeff was, it was apparent those mules were getting leg-weary. Apparently the raiders had kept to the mountains, which any raider in his right mind would have done, and judging from the look of the mules, the raiders had allowed the animals to rest on the way—probably in the shank of the night when anyone who knew wily livestock would realize full well how mules especially could take advantage of darkness if they were given half a chance, to simply turn off through the trees and hide.

Jeff grimly smiled to himself. Talador's solicitous care to arrive down here with all the mules, while motivated of a certainty by the fact that he wanted to sell every single one of the mules, had also made it possible for Ben and Jeff to get all their stolen animals back without having to do any back-tracking through the hills and forests. Providing, of course, they were able to rescue the mules, and not wind up buried in two separate mounds of stones up in here where no one would find their bodies for many years.

Once Jeff was entirely satisfied about the mules, their course and eventual destination, he put all that out of his mind and concentrated exclusively upon the slouched horseman slogging it down through the rocks on a head-hung horse. Neither one of them, the mount under the raider, or the raider himself, looked in very good shape, so evidently Talador had also had his men take positions as sentries back up through the mountains on the drive over here.

Jeff got down through the rocks as far as he dared go, sat down to remove his boots and without a sound went another few yards until he was in the smaller boulders at the edge of the trail. Now, all he had to do was wait, and hope he would be undetected until the messenger was close enough so that it would not matter if the raider's tired horse detected the gamy scent of someone hiding beside the trail.

He eased his carbine aside, loosened the Colt on his hip, hoped very hard he would not have to use either of them because of the unmistakable noise they made, and craned out as far as he dared to see the oncoming rider.

He did not see him. In fact it was several minutes before he even heard him, but by then the horse was probably only a few hundred feet up the trail so Jeff eased back very gently, looked around to make certain he was undetected, then got into position to spring upon this man as he had done before when he had also waylaid Hank Armstrong.

This time, though, it was going to be very different. He could sense that when he got back upon a round man-sized boulder which was protected to the north by a couple of even larger and taller spires. When he landed this time the man who would fall with him would not land on grassy soil; up in here there was very little grass because the land was flaked-off ancient stone packed as hard as cement. Up in this place to do what Jeff meant to attempt could very easily result in someone being injured—seriously injured.

He thought of that only indirectly; he was quite confident that this time the man he attacked would also be dumbfounded just long enough for Jeff to ride him to the ground upon the far side of the horse. That was how it had worked with Hank Armstrong.

The oncoming horse began to drag steel shoes over flint and shale-stone. Jeff, with only sound to go by because the same pinnacles which hid him from northward view also cut him off from seeing up in that direction. But the horse made a distinct sound with each step as he approached.

Jeff crouched. He heard rein-chains, then he heard leather rubbing over leather and eased low and crouched in the poised position to launch himself. The horse's head and neck appeared, its saddle and rider came into sight—and Jeff hurled himself.

This time, though, the man was wiry, and tired or not he was as wary as a hawk. He was not looking in Jeff's direction until after Jeff had launched himself, then something made the Apache turn, and although Jeff was in mid-flight, the raider acted with lightning-like reflexes. He tried to drop forward at the same moment he hung both heels into the sides of his mount. Jeff had reached for the Indian when the horse responded to being gigged so abruptly and jumped ahead. It was very close but not quite close enough. Jeff had two handfuls of Apache raider as momentum carried him on across the saddle and beyond.

He took the Indian with him in much the same manner as a fish-hawk used in carrying away its prey in both talons. He took the wiry Indian with him on across the horse and over into clear space on the far side, while the astonished and panicked horse summoned all the power he had left and bolted dead-ahead on down the rocky trail.

The Indian's co-ordination was just about perfect.

He knew in a fraction of a second what the result would be if he allowed the large white man to ride him down into the rocks.

He tried in mid-air, to twist his body in order to get Jeff headed into the rocks first, but he was neither heavy enough to accomplish this, nor did he have sufficient time.

Jeff nonetheless lost a little initiative, and when they came down the Indian was not beneath him, but was almost entirely beside him. They struck and fell and rolled, then both of them with one mind bounced up to their feet.

The Indian had a sixgun round his middle but he reached to the left side of his shellbelt for the holstered big knife there, and Jeff reached for the man's left wrist, locked his fingers around it, drew the hand up very slowly with the knife in it, forced it even higher, then swung his leg up and around and by exerting all his strength brought the knife-wrist down across his upraised leg. He heard the bone snap, saw the knife fall among the rocks, whirled his adversary who was easily forty pounds lighter and almost a full foot shorter, and pinned the raider to an upright rounded rock with one hand while he disarmed the man with his other hand.

The Indian wilted, probably from the pain of that broken wrist. The fight went out of him, and as he was forced back in an arching posture against the rock, he attempted to use his right knee to the groin but Jeff was ready, was twisting so that when the knee struck it hit hip-bone.

Then Jeff swore and swung. The Apache went six inches into the air off the ground and tumbled back downward into a heap.

9

TACTICS

There was no way to overtake and capture the Apache's mount; like most ill-treated animals this one took fullest advantage of being free and did not even pause to glance back once he no longer had a rein-hand to guide him. He was down-country and still running the last sight of him Jeff had.

But his owner was less fortunate. Jeff leaned and propped up the Indian and tried to revive him without any success. In the end he swore about having to do it, pitched the limp Indian over his shoulder, and started back.

He rested four times and the last time was when he heard men yelling as they hazed loose-stock up the funnel canyon, by then he was across the tops and coming down gingerly upon the far, eastward, side of the trap-canyon where he had left Ben and their other prisoner.

Ben stared but Armstrong's look of astonishment was much greater as Jeff sloughed off his limp Indian with the swelling wrist and arm.

Ben leaned, flopped the Indian over and searched him. Aside from a fishline wrapped carefully around a fish-hook, some silver from both sides of the border, a small pressed-flat piece of ancient paper with illegible writing upon it, the Apache had nothing of importance.

Ben straightened up as he said, "The man speaks English, if he don't have a written message on him." Then Ben looked at the swollen wrist. But he said nothing. Hank Armstrong had nothing to say either. Hank, who had not really feared Jeff right from the start of his captivity, looked from the battered man on the ground to Jeff and back to the Indian again. There were several indications that the man Hank had always thought was a pleasant, non-violent individual, was actually not much different from his partner, the other freighter.

They loaded the Indian, got astride and went very gingerly eastward with Hank leading again. He turned out to be just as nervous about detection now as he had been earlier. And it helped, that for a man who had pretended to know so little about this foothill territory, he actually knew it very well. Hank led them away with hills behind them. He said again and again, they were riding straight into the maw of hell, or something like that and Ben, who had got tired of his groaning before, did not say anything this time. He was concentrating on the way they were riding in order not to be seen.

Their Indian came round before they reached their next stop. They halted and Jeff pushed the man upright in front of him on the saddle. The Apache did not look very old but in fact his boyish appearance was deceptive, he was easily as old as any of the other men. But his arm was extremely painful, which became very clear as they continued riding and he held it in such a manner as to minimize the jars and jolts. He looked longest at Constable Armstrong but said nothing. Even when Ben or Jeff tried to talk to him the Apache acted as though he did not understand, which of course was simply not true. They all spoke English. Some were more fluent in Spanish, but they all understood English and all of them could converse in it.

Armstrong finally pointed to a wide, shallow wooded place which seemed to be the broad base of an ancient river, and would have gone down there but Ben growled at him.

"We're going to stay above ground, you idiot. Anyone could bottle us up down in there."

Hank protested. "I wasn't suggesting that we stay down in there. Only that there's water down there and these horses sure need a drink."

Ben offered no additional dissent so they descended one of the game trails, dismounted and slipped the bridles so the animals could tank up, and afterwards they led the horses over beyond the trees to the east side of the broad arroyo where they would be less likely to be discovered. There, Jeff rolled a smoke, lit it and offered it to the Apache, who glared at Jeff from jet-black, constantly-moving eyes. Jeff shrugged and lit the smoke for himself.

Ben spoke in Spanish and the Indian half turned away from Ben to watch Hank Armstrong, who was gnawing off a corner of his plug-tobacco. The Apache held out his good hand and Hank passed over the tobacco. The Indian tore off another corner, pouched it into his cheek and handed back the plug, all without a word being said. Then he ruminated and Ben almost smiled. He had never seen a *chewing* Apache before although he had seen plenty of *smoking* Apaches.

Evidently the Indian was more curious about his captors than they were about him, because after he had chewed for a while he turned and studied each of them individually. Finally, using accented but adequate English, he addressed Hank Armstrong.

"I know you. You lawman from Gila."

Hank neither confirmed it nor denied it, he simply worked on the cud in his cheek and dolefully hunkered there gazing dispassionately at the Indian.

He gestured. "These men your posse?"

"These men," stated Ben very dryly, "are the men who own those mules you bastards raided out of a canvas-camp over on the Mescal River above Lincoln."

The Indian stared at Ben. Clearly, he was astonished. "How you got over here so fast?" he asked, and Ben pointed to the discoloration starting up on the man's broken wrist. "You stretch that out here," he told the Indian, "and don't cry out like a little kid, and I'll set it for you and wrap it."

The Apache looked suspiciously at Ben. He seemed unwilling to be touched, which caused no disappointment in Ben who turned and blew smoke in the direction of his partner, acting as though he had not made the offer.

"Did you see them corral the livestock?" he asked, and Jeff shook his head.

"Nope. Didn't want to hang around over there too long. There are seven of them."

"Did you see Talador?"

Jeff had no idea whether he had seen the famous raider or not. "All I saw was our mules—all seventeen head of them."

"Eighteen."

"Seventeen, damn it. Remember, we saw old Sidney before we got very far south of Lincoln."

Ben remembered. "Excuse me. All seventeen then." He turned and looked back at their Indian. "You got a woman and kids?"

The Apache stared from unblinking black eyes. He seemed to be trying to anticipate the purpose behind everything Ben said to him. This time, when he decided he knew what Ben had in mind, he nodded his head.

Ben sighed. "You son of a bitch," he said, and lifted out his sixgun and cocked it. "You tell us how many children you got."

This time the Indian had no difficulty at all in finding his tongue. "Two kids. Two boys. Small yet."

"And a woman?"

"Yes. And a woman."

Ben looked almost pleased as he rested the cocked Colt in his lap as he sat upon the ground and motioned for the Apache to do the same.

"Where is Talador?" he asked.

The Indian raised his uninjured arm and pointed in the direction of that box canyon. "With mules." Then the Indian dropped his good arm into his lap and sat studying the man with the weapon in his fist. "You own those mules?"

Ben solemnly inclined his head.

"You want to try and get them back?" asked the Indian.

Again Ben inclined his head, gravely. "Yeah, we want to get them back. Any ideas?"

The Indian did not answer, but after a time he looked towards the far-away foothills where he and his companions had just emerged, and said, "You go.

You head back up through the trees and go west or Talador will barbecue you. You go now."

Ben ignored the warning. "Stick that busted arm out here, and take off your shirt."

The Indian opened his shirt first. His upper body was scarred and lined and as wiry as sawgrass. When he leaned to push out the injured arm he raised caustic eyes to Ben.

"If you don't go away from here they will find you," he warned.

"How?" asked Ben, leaning to reholster his Colt, then leaning forward to look at the badly swollen wrist.

"You left fresh tracks. Talador always has his riders go completely around, maybe for a half-mile, to read the sign. Talador will read it where you knocked me off the horse. He will start scouting and he will follow your sign, then surround you and shoot you to death."

"Nice, cheerful cuss," said Armstrong, but the Apache ignored Hank and crooked up a lop-sided mirthless smile as he also said, "Pretty soon now. We always corral the livestock first, then ride far out and all around. They will come soon now."

Ben looked up. "First you don't talk, then you talk all the time. Shut up and quit wiggling."

He could not make more of a bandage than he did, but it was good enough. Tight enough too, the Indian complained afterwards as he sat there flexing his fingers. He said, "You go. You better go. I tell you that. Go now."

Ben's retort effectively silenced the Indian. "Oh shut up, you lousy mule-thief. I got half a notion to hang you. Hang every blessed one of you."

To the Apache death was no stranger, but like just about every other Indian, the prospect of being hanged by the neck until he died was a grisly and chilling prospect. Nearly all tribesmen viewed that kind of demise as a disgrace and some of them held the view that if they were to die like that their souls would spend most of eternity wandering in the outer darkness.

The Indian said, "You want the mules?"

Ben looked back at the smaller man. "Why do you think we out-rode you to get over here first? You bet we want our mules back. And we'll either get them back or we'll wipe out a bunch of thieving bastards!"

The Apache nodded his head as though this was exactly the reply he had expected. "You will die," he told Ben. "They will kill you . . . but if you want to try and get mules loose, you go down near the front of the canyon."

Armstrong cursed with feeling. "Don't you do it. Don't you listen to this son of a bitch. If you go anywhere near the lower end of the canyon—that's where those renegades camp each time they come over here because the lower end of the canyon is the only place that needs guarding. Mules can't get out no place else but down there. I'll tell you what this treacherous little runt is up to—he's trying to be sly and get us down there to be killed."

Ben looked at the Indian. "Sure," he said softly, as though Armstrong had not spoken. "Sure, we'll go down there . . . You and Constable Armstrong—my partner and me behind you. Stand up!"

The Indian arose but slowly, his eyes fixed to Ben Hurley. He seemed to anticipate what Armstrong did not understand until some time after he had also been ordered to rise.

The Indian said, "You won't make it. You are wrong to try it."

Armstrong looked at Ben, then at Jeff, and gradually his expression underwent a complete change. "A bushwhack," he groaned aloud. "You're going to set up a bushwhack using me and this rag-head as bait."

Ben said nothing but he gestured for the pair of prisoners to move back through to the far side of the trees again, over where the narrow little warm-water creek was meandering.

Jeff took their livestock farther back where the chance of an accidental discovery was just about nil, then he hobbled the beasts, removed their saddles, and hurried back to arrive by the creek just as Ben told Armstrong to shut up.

The Indian accepted the possibility that he might indeed become bait for the white men, but he did not accept it stoically. Very few Indians were ever stoics; they were inveterate schemers, and this particular variety of Indian was the most treacherous of the entire South-west. Ben had no illusions. Neither did anyone else who had ever lived around Apaches.

They did not go back through the foothills the way they had previously come over to the wide arroyo, they instead walked more southward, but they still utilized all the shelter they could find.

Armstrong's shirt darkened with sweat. The Apache moving along at his side was already shirtless, and he normally shone greasily anyway, so it was impossible to say whether his reaction was also fear. He could not escape. They did not come close to any kind of covert, but his small, obsidian eyes were never still. He reminded Jeff Hill of a condemned man on his way to the stone wall or the gallows with nothing to lose whether he broke and ran for it or whether he didn't run for it.

But Jeff had no desire to cut loose with gunfire and

evidently this was also in his partner's mind because although Ben strode along with his carbine in both hands and inches from the Indian, Ben was in more of a position to brain the Indian than to shoot him.

Once, the Apache looked back. Ben growled and touched him with the Winchester and the Indian did not turn again.

But he finally said, "If they kill us, they will kill you too. I tell you there is a way to get those mules out of the canyon."

Jeff and Ben were instantly interested but Armstrong snarled at the Apache. "He's a lousy liar. There ain't no way to get animals out of there except down through the gate."

Jeff punched the lawman in the back and told him to be quiet. Then he and Ben waited for the Indian to speak again. It was not a very long wait.

"There is a crack in the rock wall on this side," the Apache stated. "Men filled it with rocks many years ago. I remember. In those days I was very young and my people used the canyon when they brought horses up out of Mexico. They kept them down in there, and one night a whole herd escaped and the men found that big narrow slot where the wall had broken away. They went down there and worked all day until they filled the crack with stones."

Ben brushed the Indian with his gunbarrel. "Lead us up there, and I sure hope you're not lying."

The Indian instantly changed course, walking northward. Armstrong showed relief on his face for the first time. They were now trudging away from the lower end of the canyon.

Evidently the mules were now corralled because it was quiet. No one was yelling over through the rocks where the canyon was. It was also getting along to-

wards that time of day when people who had com-
pleted their labour took *siestas,* had naps through the
middle of the day, or at least through the hottest part
of the day, except that in the springtime the days were
not really as uncomfortably hot over here as they
would become another month or two to come.

Jeff leaned and said, "Ben; if there's no slot up
here, that little rag-head bastard has led us a long
way northward and we'll still have to go down yonder
to get the mules out."

Ben had already made this identical conclusion.
"But if there is a slot, and if we can get it un-
plugged . . . Down there where the gate is, Jeff, we'd
have one hell of a battle on our hands if they didn't
fall for the trick of using Hank and the raider to bait
them out to us."

They exchanged a look, then said no more but
trudged along in the shade which was now forming in
their side of the funnel-canyon.

10

SWEAT AND DUST—AND FEAR

There *was* a slot, and the reason it had been invisible from over across the canyon where they had originally spied out this place was because of two trees and some underbrush which had evidently been planted there many years ago to further strengthen this one weakness of the entire box-canyon.

The Indians who had piled stones in the breach had done a good job. Now, so many years later, there was even an occasional tuft of bunch-grass growing between the layers of rock.

Without a word Jeff pushed Armstrong ahead with him, and growled an order. "Lift 'em out and don't drop 'em. Lift them down out of there and set them to one side. Get to work!"

The Apache was worthless with his broken wrist. He remained to one side, watching, sometimes grinning over Hank Armstrong's sweaty discomfort. It was clear that if Armstrong had ever done much actual physical labour it had been many years earlier.

Ben helped, but he was wary of the Indian and

rarely took his eyes off the Apache for more than a moment or two at a time.

But the Indian seemed disinclined to break and run for it. Probably because if he had done this the only route open to him was northward, up the nearly vertical side of the stone wall, which closed in the box-canyon, and his captors could pick him off as readily as shooting fish in a rainbarrel—and he knew it.

They worried a little about someone coming up into this upper end of the canyon. At least Armstrong worried a lot about that, even though Ben scoffed and was of the opinion that the raiders would by now be all asleep—except a sentinel—down in the shaded part of the canyon where the gate was.

They had to work constantly. The sun shifted, passed beyond them and before they were midway down with the rocks it had completely traversed the open area above the funnel-canyon.

The work was not only hard, it was also hot work. They got thirsty and had no water. They would have enjoyed a respite to perhaps have a relaxing smoke. They could not do that either.

Finally, they had enough rocks out of the way to step across into the canyon. Jeff shoved the Indian through first. Then he and Ben growled at Armstrong and when all of them were in the canyon they saw the mules, and if ever animals looked tired and dusty and thirsty, it was their livestock.

Ben's face settled into a murderous expression. He was like many other stockmen, a deadly enemy to people who neglected or abused good-using livestock. "I'd like to slip down and shoot me some rag-heads," he muttered. Jeff had no comment. He turned back to the slot, studied it, then said, "Ben, if you want to slip down and get below them I'll finish making the passageway usable."

He took Armstrong and the Indian back out through and told the Apache where to stand as he and Armstrong returned to work. When they had the slot open it was about two feet wide and with somewhat hazardous footing unless animals were careful—which a mule could be relied upon to be; there was no more surefooted beast in all Creation in the rocks than a mule.

The Indian hissed and pointed with his good hand. He seemed to be as interested in this affair as anyone else. The least interested man was Constable Armstrong and when the first big dun mule walked over, looked through, then picked his way to come out of the canyon, Jeff grinned and said, "Hell, Abe. Sure nice to see your long darned face again."

The mules were quietly hazed northward. By the time the last mule was out of the canyon and Ben appeared, Jeff was anxious to get back for the horses. He took the Indian with him and left Armstrong to help his partner line out their mules towards the higher country out back, where they could then be driven eastward roughly in the direction of either Gila or, more north-easterly, in the direction of Lincoln.

The Apache trotted beside Jeff grinning widely. He did not say a word, not even when they got back to the horses and he could only stand by while Jeff did the saddling, and when Jeff asked him where the trackers were he had said Talador always sent them out right after corralling stolen livestock.

In fact he said nothing even when they were astride heading back, but he continued to look as though being part of a successful deception even when it was against his own companions, pleased him very much.

They made good time. If the raiders down in the

shade of the lower canyon had been watchful at all they would have seen those two, but they didn't, and whether this was understandable or not, it was a disaster for the thieves who had worked so hard and so long getting their stolen mules over this far.

Once, when they turned to follow mule-sign where Ben and Hank were on foot, the Indian looked around and said, "Someone is coming from Verde Wells." He sounded pleased about this. Maybe he was, but if so he hadn't used much sense in pointing out the dust to his captor, because Jeff urged the horses ahead with more haste, found Armstrong and Ben, got them aboard their saddles, then they hurried at getting the mules on around the canyon and strung out for home.

That dust which the Indian had pointed out did not seem to be the product of very many riders. In fact Ben was of the opinion that it was being made by a buggy, not by riders at all.

But they could not be sure. They did not in fact ever get to see who was making that dust as they swung the tired mules around the headland above the box-canyon and allowed them to pick their own way down through the rocks towards the lower country which was between them and Gila. Out there, there were very few rocks and no fields of huge ones at all. In fact all that southward country was open. Even the interludes of shelter were few and far between. It was good country to make time in, except that both the mules and the saddlestock were just about worn down.

From here on if they had to make a race of it, and providing their pursuers were mounted on fresh animals, they were doomed.

But as they trickled down out of the rocks and emerged into the hot, open, almost totally flat territory, they did not see a soul behind them or over to the south-east where the funnel-canyon had its cor-ralled-off mouth.

They trotted, which was the best gait they could use for making time when all their animals were used up. They trotted for two miles than halted to let the animals "blow" and out here the Indian made a big gesture with his good arm. "They should be in sight," he said, not acting very disappointed that they weren't. "They should have found your sign by now." He dropped his signalling hand and spat amber, then said, "They are tired men."

Ben was a little doughty about that. "Who isn't a tired man? Head 'em out and get 'em moving again." But as the mules picked up the trail again Ben went over to the Apache, rode stirrup and said, "Let him down, Jeff." His partner did not even hesitate, he shoved the Indian off his saddle, off his horse, and rode on, leaving Ben back there looking earthward from his horse as he said, "Go on back, rag-head."

The Indian's black eyes never left Ben's face. "I turn and run, you shoot me in the back."

Ben didn't deny it, he simply said, "Go on—turn back and move out."

For a moment longer they regarded one another then the Apache turned, leaned and broke over into that odd little pigeon-toed trot his people used so tirelessly.

Ben looped his reins, rolled and lit a smoke, watched the Indian for a few minutes, then turned and loped after his partner and their mules.

It did not seem possible to do what they had done. He made a derisive snort about the legendary clever-ness of Talador. Hell! two dog-tired freighters had out-smarted the cleverest Apache of the low-desert.

He rode along looking back, his confidence and

assurance growing by the second. He was certain, without recalling the Indian's comment, about why Talador had not found them and had been unable to effectively pursue them. His riders were tired, but their mounts were much more so. The riders might have been able to withstand another day of hard-riding, and even a fight, but their horses could not do that.

He considered his own animal, the mount of his partner, and the lawman from Gila. He also considered the condition of their mules. None of them were in very good shape. The best of the lot was the mount under Hank Armstrong. He had not covered as much ground as the other animals or he would not have been holding up was well as he appeared to be.

They turned slightly more southward, sent aloft a pale streamer of dust and headed directly for the vicinity of Gila. Ben rode up to Jeff to suggest that they halt there long enough to water and grain the animals before pushing onward. Jeff was agreeable. He was also speculating about just how much longer their horses and mules could keep this up even with an hour's rest, some water, and a decent bait of rolled barley.

Ben's comment was succinct and had little to do with how much longer they kept it up. He simply said, "It's a hell of a choice but it's not up to us. If we lie over more than about an hour Talador will probably show up. We'd lose our lead, and right now that's about all that's going to keep us alive."

Jeff jerked a thumb. "How about him; let him loose in Gila?"

Ben shrugged. "We can use an extra hand on up to Lincoln," he said, and they grinned at each other.

By the time they had Gila in sight the mules were

down to a slogging walk. They were gaunt and sunken-eyed and worn-down, but they kept moving almost as though, hard as this was, they understood what the alternative would be if Talador caught up.

When they were approaching the outskirts of the village Ben smiled over at Hank Armstrong. "We'll take on water and grain here, then keep going . . . You too."

Armstrong, who had visible personal proof that what he had thought could not be accomplished by a pair of freighters, had in fact been accomplished, was still pessimistic. "It's not goin' to help a hell of a lot," he told Ben, and looked apprehensively back. "Maybe Talador couldn't make it now, but you can bet your boots he'll be along, and when he does . . . !"

"No wonder you're such a louse," Ben said, looking the lawman squarely in the eye. "You're gutless and on top of that you don't have any confidence." He pointed. "Is that the Gila liverybarn, that long shed at the north end of town?"

"No, that's an old abandoned barracks—and you'd ought to know it because you had your horses at the other end of town. . . . You're just trying to trap me some way."

Ben nodded affirmatively because that had been exactly what he'd had in mind; he wanted to bait the constable into turning treacherous. He wanted to know whether Armstrong was going to make trouble here in Gila or not.

He still was not certain as they drifted the mules around the village towards its lower end, and could see a few people, mostly men, craning from the back-alley at the arrival of a dusty, tucked-up band of driven animals with equally as worn and disreputable-looking drovers. They were unable to identify their own constable as being one of the drovers until the drovers brought their willing charges to a milling halt in the shaded big yard of the liverybarn. The mules went at once to the muddy area around the stone trough, unmindful of a horde of hornets and mud-daubers who were usually on patrol around there.

The youthful Mexican did not come out if indeed he was in the barn, but an older hostler approached, recognized the lawman and became more confident as he walked up and said, "Nice mules, Hank. You got an interest in them?"

Armstrong did not return the hostler's smile. He in fact squinted downward wearing a vinegary expression when he said, "I expect a man could say I got an interest in 'em, Lewis. These here are freighters from over at Lincoln. It's their mules. We just—found 'em in a box-canyon some miles north-west of here."

Lewis's smile faded and his eyes widened. "Not up in the blasted foothills?"

"Yas, up in the damned foothills," stated irritable Hank Armstrong.

Lewis looked from Ben to Jeff, then over to the lawman again. "You aren't supposed—no one's supposed to go up in there, Hank. It's a bad place."

Jeff leaned and said, "We've heard that, friend, but Hank here—he's a fearless feller, and he showed us exactly how to find our mules up there. I'd say old Hank's about the most savvy, bravest constable around, wouldn't you?"

Lewis did not reply. He looked a long while at Armstrong then walked away making a slight cluck-ing sound. Ben kneed his horse over to bar Lewis's return to the barn runway.

"We need a quart of barley all around, out here,"

he informed Lewis, and fished in a pocket to flip a gold coin earthward.

Old Lewis was on that coin almost before it had settled in the dust, then he scuttled away in haste yelling a Mexican name.

"Juan Sunday! Juan Sunday! Hey, John Domingo get your lazy tail out here we got work to do!"

The Mexican who eventually walked into sight was also older. Ben had expected it to be the youthful dayman, but instead it was a heavy-set, very dark and coarse-faced Mexican. If he understood English, which he probably did, he never spoke it. But he went to work at once lugging feed-boxes to the yard where Lewis was wheeling a barrow full of rolled barley.

The loose-stock was in no hurry to leave the shade nor the water, nor this place where they did not have to move unless they wanted to, so the moment they caught a scent of grain they turned from the water-trough, abandoning it to the mud-daubers again, and began pushing and shoving around the pair of harassed and sweating liverymen.

Jeff and Ben filled their hats with grain and went back to feed their saddle-stock, and afterwards loosen the cinches for a few minutes, remove the bridles and let the horses drink, eat grain, and rest.

There was still plenty of heat in the day even though there was also a collection of diverse shadows forming here and there.

Up the short road of the village wary townsmen seemed disinclined to go any closer to the liverybarn-yard than they were as they stood in front of several buildings, craning and speculating. They lived in a harsh environment which was inhabited by fierce horsemen. Those dirty, sunken-eyed individuals down

in the tree-shaded liverybarn-yard looked like villainous rustlers at the very best, and murderous aliens at
the worst.

Curiosity was one thing, but perhaps risking one's
life just for a closer look, was something else.

No one even approached although they could all
very clearly distinguish their township-lawman down
there. Not everyone was convinced Armstrong was a
local hero, in any case.

Once, someone looked rearward and pointed to a
distant dust-banner. The men at the liverybarn had
also seen that tell-tale indication of others on their
way to Gila, and were sitting their saddles again,
stonily watching. Whoever was far back was not
coming at a dead run, that much was obvious by the
slowness with which the dust-banner was moving.
Still, the men at the liverybarn preferred not to sacri-
fice any more of their advantageous head-start than
they had to, so as they watched the mules finish the
last of the barley, they clucked them up into movement, started them on out around the barn and out
across the slightly more brushy countryside on towards
the north-west. The two freighters also seemed to be
herding Gila's lawman along with the mules.

11

HANK ARMSTRONG

Armstrong did not object, partly because in all probability he had anticipated having to help with the drive beyond his local bailiwick, partly because he was apprehensive. If that was Talador back yonder making that dust from the north-east, it would probably be just as well if Armstrong were not in Gila when the raiders arrived, and after they arrived and were told Armstrong was indeed riding with the men from Lincoln, there could be no doubt at all about how much better it would be for Hank Armstrong if he was a long way off and still going.

Like it or not, Constable Armstrong's lot had been put in with the lot of the freighters from Lincoln and as they left Gila heading towards the more brushy and overgrown territory on westerly, he took it upon himself to keep a sharp watch rearward.

Ben and Jeff grinned about that. Armstrong had been almost a nervous wreck before there was any indication of pursuit. Now, he was worse off than ever. But his vigil was in the favour of the owners of the mules and for that reason even when Armstrong seemed to want to drop back a little, the freighters did not harass him. Their earlier anxiety over his willingness to escape ceased to exist. Armstrong was now between a rock and a hard place, and he knew it. The freighters, unfriendly though they were, could not even be classified in the same category as someone as murderously savage as Talador and his raiders—deadly men, every man-jack of them.

The mules benefited from their respite back at Gila and their owners preferred to utilize this renewed strength without burning it all up in a few wild rushes; they let the mules walk for a mile, then eased them over into a trot and held them to it for two more miles before allowing them to walk again. Like that, they could cover three times the miles they would be able to cover in a dead run under a hot but fading sun.

The saddle-horses too were better off after their grain and water and rest.

It was Jeff's opinion that in the long run it would prove out that they had not actually sacrificed any of their lead after all. He based this suggestion upon what he considered Talador's inevitable halt back at Gila, too. His horses and men were just as much—maybe even more—in need of a rest when they arrived at a place like Gila where they could slack off for a little while—maybe an hour or two.

Ben thought this was about right but Hank, looking over his shoulder, was of the opinion that if they got to thinking like this and eased off, some time in the oncoming night they would probably be overtaken.

"Naw," contradicted Jeff. "If we change course they won't even be able to hear us, and that's about their only way to keep track of us once it gets dark."

They rarely agreed with Armstrong but his excessive

caution was in their favour, which they understood and appreciated as they trotted for a seemingly endless period of time in and out of the underbrush, and actually made better time than they had expected to make. They would still be unable to get very close to Lincoln before nightfall, but it was reassuring to realize that the next day, unless something highly untoward occurred, they would be back along the Mescal River.

In fact, by the time the first long shadows of full dusk arrived they were close enough to the coach-road lying southward from Lincoln to expect to reach it before nightfall, and for once even Hank Armstrong showed a little optimism. When he could stand in his stirrups and watch the first mules on ahead reach the roadway and automatically turn northward out of long habit, he settled back down and said, "By golly—there's a chance. A slim one by gawd, but still a chance that we'll make it." And this possibility seemed to trigger a fresh worry because he promptly turned and said, "And what kind of gratitude will you fellers dispose?"

Jeff wrinkled his forehead. "What?"

"Well, damn it all, I showed you how to get your mules back didn't I? And I he'ped you do it, and showed you how to slip around Talador, and how to make it all the way back to Gila didn't I? And I hung right in there doin' my best when the goin' was worst, didn't I? And I'm over here, ain't I, still doing everything I can do to make sure you boys get back to safety."

Jeff slowly wagged his head. "I had no idea," he replied, "how much you did to help us. By golly I'm beginning to think we never could have made it except for you."

Armstrong glared. "Well, for a lousy fact, gents, you couldn't have made it."

"It wasn't you," put in Ben, "who showed us how to get the mules back, it was that runty little rag-head."

"Yeah? Who showed you that lousy canyon in the first place and who figured it so's you'd know exactly how Talador would behave once he got down there? You better believe it, gents, without me you'd never have been able to bring it off."

"And if you hadn't got too anxious, we wouldn't have caught you trying to sneak past to warn that louse neither," stated Ben. "If it was put to a vote, Hank, I'd vote to shoot you as soon as we're on the outskirts of Lincoln."

Armstrong looked very bitter, perhaps with some reason, but probably with nowhere nearly as much reason as he thought. Nonetheless, he said no more and kept the mules moving, along with Ben and Jeff, until the last animal turned northward up the coach-road. By then it was beginning to pass from dusk to soft nightfall.

They could not see the lights of Lincoln yet, but it was reassuring for some obscure reason to realize that they were this close. Yesterday at this time their chances of even getting out of Lem Steele's foothills alive, had seemed very near to an impossibility. They felt good and were entitled to feel good.

But they didn't look very good; they were soiled and shrunken, unshaven and gritty-eyed; someone coming unexpectedly upon them in the night would have been positive they were in the presence of the most degraded variety of renegades.

This no doubt had something to do with Hank Armstrong's reaction to them. They appeared to be the kind of men who were fully capable of killing him on the outskirts of Lincoln.

He chewed tobacco, rode along slouched and morose, and from time to time observed his riding companions, who now seemed less inclined to ride with him than they had been earlier in the day—and that also preyed on his thoughts.

Finally, Ben pointed far off and said, "The lights of town, by gawd."

He was correct, but they appeared as little more than pinpricks of orange brilliance in the warm, moonless night, many miles onward.

Ben and Jeff, who knew every foot of this roadway from below the line in Mexico all the way up to Animas and the Utah line, turned their walking mules off the coach-road for a mile hike westerly where the Mescal had a little tributary. They had camped over there a hundred times, at least, over the past half dozen or so years. When they reached the willows and pushed through into the lush-grass little meadow next to the watercourse, Hank registered surprise that such a hidden place existed.

There was sign on all sides where freighters had camped so evidently Ben and Jeff were not the only ones who knew of this place. And their mules, footsore by now despite being shod, fanned out to graze at once. They too were in familiar territory once again.

They off-saddled and made their camp with Armstrong feeling safe for the first time. He said Talador would never find this place in the darkness and he was correct.

For supper each freighter had a smoke and the lawman had a fresh cud of tobacco. It was a warm night, but even so they spread their blankets upon the grass. They were very tired men, all three of them.

"Any wolves or cougars or bears over here?" asked the lawman. "If these darned mules get stampeded to the four winds by varmints me and my horse ain't up to doing it all over again."

"Nothing like that over here," yawned Jeff. "They don't even have a dishonest sheriff over here. And you got to admit that's sure unusual."

Armstrong offered no such admission at all. In fact he turned up on to his side so he would not have to look at his companions.

Ben snored. It was not a pretty sound but on the other hand it lacked the wet, bubbly, deep-down raspiness of most snorers.

Jeff lay back until he finished his smoke, then he hauled up an ancient army blanket to cover his fully-attired body and breathed with an even and rhythmic sweep.

For a long time Hank Armstrong simply listened. Chewed his cud and scowled in concentration, and simply listened. He was a very careful man.

He was so cautious in fact that he did not move for a solid hour after the freighters had dropped back on their bedrolls. But eventually he turned very slowly, without making a sound, and for another ten minutes he watched both the men lying nearby.

He needed a usable gun in order to accomplish very much even though the freighters were lying there as inert as corpses, because he had seen them in action and respected their numbers. Either one of them would have been a handful but both of them together . . . He leaned a little, got an arm propped into place and raised his upper body very carefully. Then he used both hands pressing flat to hoist himself into a crouched position, and at that moment Jeff Hill sighed, cleared his throat, and with his left hand carelessly flung aside the blanket. His right hand was holding a cocked sixgun. The weapon was lying atop the freighter's middle and although it was not pointing directly at Hank, it was pointing in his general direction.

Jeff resumed his deep-down, rhythmic breathing.

Hank scarcely breathed for ten seconds, then he started to move again, but this time to draw back, to turn and with great care, to move away. He finally was able to get to his feet and tiptoe across the sound-deadening green grass in the direction of the hobbled saddle-stock.

He could of course have taken his own horse and the other two, which were also hobbled, or at the very least he could have spooked the other two so that if the freighters awakened they would be unable to effect an immediate pursuit. That would have been the wise thing to do.

Instead, Armstrong saddled his own animal, did not go near the freighters' animals, walked his horse out a dozen or so yards before mounting it, and after that walked it very carefully another hundred yards, westerly, which was the direction he continued in until there was no sight of him at all.

Ben raised up a little. "Did he do it?" he asked, and Jeff, still lying with that cocked Colt on his middle, eased down the hammer as he replied.

"Yup. The son of a bitch went and did it, and unless he gets silly we've seen the last of Mister Armstrong. I figure Talador and the folks over at Gila had also seen the last of him. I guess we'd ought to be ashamed, messing up his career like we did. Ruinin' his prospects over at Gila, and spoiling his contact with the lousy raiders."

Ben yawned again. "I'm ashamed, are you?"

"Just go back to sleep," replied Jeff, "And if you keep up that snoring I'm going to ram a fistful of grass in your mouth."

Evidently Constable Armstrong, wherever he went in the night, chose not to approach even within hearing distance of his two former companions again because when Jeff and Ben awakened in the morning there was no sign of him and their mules, which were normally highly sensitive to scents and sounds, had detected nothing after Armstrong's departure. The mules were still dozing when their owners rolled out, stiffly, and got to their feet in the dawn chill, more gaunt than ever.

"Three more hours," Jeff said, as they were saddling up.

The horses were in better shape this morning than they had been in since leaving Lincoln. The mules, too, had a better outlook. They walked back to the coach-road and again turned up it.

Now, though, they could not see the town. They rode and walked another two miles before they could make out rooftops. But there was a consolation. They could not make out any more dust coming from the east. Either Talador had got no farther than Gila, or he had camped somewhere between, or maybe he had just decided to accept this first defeat of his raiding career. Neither of the freighters believed the latter possibility at all. They guessed Talador had just decided the freighters had got too much of a lead to be overtaken.

The morning stage passed them with brilliant sunshine on all sides but the cold was still enough to keep them riding hunched and glum-looking when they waved back to the whip and gunguard.

Several wagons came along, travellers heading only the Lord knew where down in this bitter territory, and they encountered an ancient Mexican in his coarse wool poncho, accompanied by his nephew a small, handsome, black-eyed youngster of maybe twelve or thirteen, shooing along ten or fifteen fat goats, clearly on their way to Lincoln to dispose of those meat animals. Probably too they expected to dispose of them among the local Mexicans because goat meat was never a favourite among *gringos*.

The old Mexican looked, looked again, then reached to draw his nephew to him and to step off the roadway, and after those filthy, sunken-eyed and unshaven *gringos* had ridden past, the old man made the sign of the cross.

Lincoln, which had appeared on the horizon of Ben and Jeff any number of times before, had never been such a welcome sight as it now was, nor had it ever looked so reassuring to them.

Ben said, "There are worse places," and Jeff agreed with that. "Yeah. Gila for one. Verde Wells for another. And don't forget Purgatory."

They finally reached the outskirts, hazed their mules into the public corrals, checked the troughs to be certain there was clean water, then they climbed stiffly from their saddles and walked into the liverybarn from out back.

There was not a soul in sight. It was either too early in the morning or perhaps the liveryman, with no reason to expect to do much business was still sleeping somewhere, possibly in his office.

Jeff groaned and said, "Wouldn't you darned well know it? Here we are, the first genuine heroes ever come through this lousy barn—and no one gives a damn."

They left their riding equipment where it was dumped, stalled their horses, forked in feed and grain, then went dourly up to the harness-room door and looked in. The fat liveryman was indeed sleeping, with a cup of cooling coffee on the table in front of him.

Ben lifted out his Colt, cocked it and fired it. The liveryman and his chair went down in a sprawling heap. He bleated at sight of those two murderous apparitions in his doorway.

Ben holstered the gun. "There are two stalled horses on the south side, mister. Wash 'em; let 'em dry in the sun, then cuff 'em, and then give 'em fresh hay but no more grain. And in the public corrals, mister, there are seventeen mules. Hay 'em but no grain. You understand?"

"Yes, sir. I sure do understand!"

Ben and Jeff turned to stroll up to the sun-bright front roadway and head over to the café. Later, they would also hunt up Drake Haslett.

12

LINCOLN AGAIN

They did not have to hunt Drake up, he came into the café before they were half through breakfast. The liveryman had hunted up Drake and had taken a solemn oath that the two men who had shot up his harness-room and nearly pitched him head-first into a heart seizure by gawd, were Frank and Jesse James because he had seen their identical pictures at least thirty times since boyhood and he'd know those two anywhere he ever saw them!

Haslett was shocked at the appearance of the breakfasting men but he was better at hiding his reactions than the liveryman had been, nor did he make such a mistake in identities either.

He signalled for coffee from the caféman, hitched his holster around and eased down at the counter beside Jeff Hill. "Got the mules back," he said, "eh?"

Jeff nodded and went right on eating. He had been hungrier in his life but right at this moment he could not remember when that had been. There was always time to talk, but eating was something which frequently required direct attention. That was what he and his partner were doing right now; paying strict attention to their meal.

Drake Haslett sipped his coffee, eyed the diners on his right, felt mild awe at the way they put away food, the amount of it they put away, and the speed with which they ate it.

"Not good for folks to eat fast," he murmured. "My maw used to tell me that, and I've heard it from other folks too. Knots up the grub in a man's entrails. Could maybe even bring on the croup."

Ben raised tawny eyes. "How's Miss Sansouci?"

Sheriff Haslett blinked, then turned a pale sort of salmon-belly pink. "Well; she's just fine, Ben. Only she's a Mrs. not a Miss."

Ben stopped masticating. "You're fooling around with a married woman?"

"Damn it—she's a widow-woman. I told you that."

"Did you?" said Ben mildly. "When; before we rode off and did your sheriffing for you and got our livestock back while you been playing Romeo with a widow-woman?"

Drake's colour deepened. He had a fierce temper. He also had a well-developed sense of guilt, when he had to have such a thing. "I told you I'd go along— right after I drummed up a decent posse and all." Drake quickly brought the subject back to what he had earlier wanted to discuss. "You got all eighteen mules back, unhurt?"

"No. Sidney's somewhere on the south desert. But we got the other seventeen." Ben went back to eating.

"What about Talador—or whoever had them?" asked the lawman. "You boys meet him?"

Jeff said, "Never saw hide nor hair." Then he proceeded to tell Sheriff Haslett about Hank Armstrong, the constable over at Gila, and Drake Haslett pursed his lips in strong disapproval. He even scowled.

"And you let him go?" he demanded, when Jeff's recitation was finished.

Ben spoke again. "Why not? You got to do something to earn your pay. He rode west, down maybe eight miles. Maybe six miles. Now's your chance to make up that posse, Drake."

Haslett sensed the sarcasm and glowered but Ben did not pay the slightest attention. He went back to his meal.

The caféman came and refilled all the coffee cups then turned and padded away in his bedroom slippers. He had once been a trail-drover. He had frozen his feet in Colorado and had never been able to do much outside work afterwards, especially in cold weather, which was why he had left the upland cattle country and had settled in lower Arizona.

Sheriff Haslett wanted details of the liberation of those stolen mules so Jeff gave it to him, blow by blow, between mouthfuls, and Ben nodded his head in affirmation from time to time but otherwise did not say a word. Not even when Drake growled over Jeff's recitation of how they released the scrawny little rag-head.

"Should have brought him in," said the lawman. "We got to put every one of those bastards out of commission or this darned raiding will go on forever."

Ben almost said something, though, when Haslett made that remark. It was the limping arrival of the caféman with two dishes of blueberry pie that kept Ben silent.

The caféman produced a key and started to place it upon the counter as he said, "You gents are welcome to use my bath-house out back. There's a fresh cake of soap out there and a towel that's only been used by a couple of travellers ahead of you. Two bits a man."

Jaff raised hostile eyes. "You sayin' we smell bad?" he demanded, and the caféman reddened and without another word turned away, still clutching his bath-house key.

Ben said, "Hey; Limpy. Leave it!" He fished out a half dollar and spun it away from him across the counter where the caféman deftly caught it and tossed back the key. He did not speak and he did not linger. Clearly, in his opinion, those two bad-smelling, filthy, gaunt, sunken-eyed bewhiskered men the sheriff had been talking to, were either gunmen or fugitives of some kind.

Ben finished first and leaned back to make a smoke. As he did this he said, "Drake; anyone been lookin' out for our canvas-camp up the river?"

Haslett cleared his throat again. "As a matter of fact I was figuring on taking a buggy-ride up that way this evening."

Ben lit up, exhaled and flipped the match away. "Alone?"

Drake frowned. "What the hell difference would that make?"

"Maybe none," said Ben. "Anyway, why don't you just saddle up and ride up there with us when we're finished bathing? That way you'll have the night to go buggy-ridin' somewhere else." Ben arose, dropped some silver beside his plate, and looked at his partner. "I'll go take the first bath," he announced.

Jeff was agreeable. "Don't stand on the towel when you are finished. Like you usually do."

Ben walked out, cigarette drooping, holstered Colt swinging, bearded, bronzed and shrunken-face hat-brim-shadowed making him look more than ever villainous.

Jeff took his time over the blueberry pie and his fourth cup of java. There was no need to hurry anyway; he wouldn't be able to use the wooden tub for a half hour. He estimated that it would require at least that much time for Ben Hurley to get the caked dirt, the dried sweat, and the layered dust and sage-pollen off himself.

He said, "Drake, you got a bad country. A bad territory around here. That dishonest lawman over at Gila wasn't the only lawman unwilling to do his job." Jeff arose as he said this, and also spilled silver beside his plate. Then he looked Haslett squarely in the face.

"Verde Wells has crooked law too."

He turned and sauntered out into the morning-sun brilliance and ten seconds later Haslett came out and said, "If you're hinting about me. . . ."

"Hinting my butt," said Jeff, and turned to leave but Drake Haslett restrained him with an outflung hand. Jeff looked down, looked up, and said, "Take that claw off me, Drake." He wasn't smiling and his voice was very soft, almost gentle.

Drake removed the hand. "All right," he muttered. "I'll be ready to ride up the river when you fellers are."

Jeff continued to study the lawman a few moments longer before turning to stroll on around the building in the direction of the bath-house.

Drake Haslett crossed to his jailhouse office not quite angry, but plenty indignant. Except that he also felt guilty. He hadn't done his job, and he could lie to himself until the blasted cows came home and he'd still know that was the plain truth.

At the bath-house when Jeff walked in Ben looked up from the steel-bound wooden tub where water as dark as soot was properly hiding two-thirds of the man the dirt had soaked off of, and said, "Where's Drake?"

"Fixing to get his horse and ride up the river with us. Why; you want him?"

"Yeah. Five yards in front when we go up there."

Jeff stared. "What the hell for?"

Ben smiled and pointed. "Light that cigar and pass it to me will you?"

Jeff obliged, savoured the taste and handed the thing to the soaking man. Ben then said, "And we'll leave the mules right here until we come back for 'em maybe tomorrow—or the next day."

Jeff pulled over an empty horseshoe keg and sat on it. "Spit it out," he ordered. "I'm not in the mood for any of your damned riddles."

Ben obliged. "You think that son of a bitch Talador is going to still be back at Gila drinking *cerbeza* and strutting up and down the roadway? Like hell he is. And whatever happened to that dust he was spreading?"

"He left it in Gila, what else?"

"He didn't leave nothin' in Gila," stated Ben. "We made him look real bad to all the Mexes and the rag-heads, and most of all to the chicken-gutted whites he's been intimidating for so long. You think he don't want to ride back to Gila with a coup-stick in his fist with your hair and mine tied to it? You darned right he does. The dust? He didn't keep comin' after us, partner. He knew where we were goin' and once he knew that, he swung northward a couple of miles so's when he reaches the river he'll be directly across from our camp. And Jeff, he knows exactly where that camp is, don't he?"

Jeff sat a long while soberly regarding his partner, who hadn't removed his hat as he'd bathed, and was now also being careful not to trickle water on the cigar he was half-smoking and half-chewing as he resumed his scrubbing, then arose in the tub and motioned for Jeff to pass him the towel, which Jeff did as he also arose and hung up his hat and peeled out of his shirt so he would at least be partially ready when his partner climbed out of the tub.

He might have used the same water but not this time. A man could almost have floated a horseshoe in it. He pulled the cork as soon as Ben climbed out, then he watched to be certain Ben did not stand on the towel as he got dressed.

Later, Ben obligingly worked the hand-pump while Jeff stripped, and although the water came directly from a dug-well, it was not cold. Neither was it hot. There was a hollow sapling outside through which all bath-water ran for two hundred feet before falling into the wooden tub. On a hot day the water reached the tub lukewarm which, so it was said, was the best kind of water for folks to bathe in. Cold water bothered the veins and arteries and whatnot, and if water was too hot, it was claimed that married men should never immerse themselves in really hot water because of the very real danger of impotency. There was a supporting argument about that. It was said President Andy Jackson bathed twice yearly in very hot water, and as folks knew, old Andy and Rachel his wife had never done very good by way of a family.

Jeff climbed into the tub, turned around twice like a cow in tall grass, then hunched up and sat down, and Ben pitched the soap in as he flicked cigar ash. "I'll go look up Drake," he told Jeff. "And make sure he don't weasel out on us."

Jeff turned. "You really believe that rag-head raider will be up there at the canvas-camp?"

"Yeah, I really believe it, and he'll bushwhack us from across the river sure as your settin' there naked as a jaybird . . . Is that a mole or dirt?"

"Get the hell out of here, and if you're so all-fired sure we're goin' to be in a fight this afternoon you'd best get Drake to make up a posse."

"He'd never do it, and if I told him what I thought he'd only say I'm crazy," retorted Ben and walked out of the bath-house neglecting to close the door until Jeff turned the air blue yelling for him to come back and close that damned door.

Jeff had no stogie so he dried his hands on his shirt-tail and made a cigarette which he smoked as he lolled and soaked, and thought.

Ben was no fool. He knew Indians about as well as Indians knew themselves. He also knew raiders and border-jumpers and mule-thieves. There had been a number of times during their long association when he'd wondered if perhaps Ben hadn't at one time or another been an outlaw.

It was one of those things a man did not ask another man regardless of how long they had known one another.

The point was, to Jeff Hill, if Ben was so confident Talador had not given up, which would have been Jeff's guess, why then the chances were great that in fact Talador had not given up.

It was a plain fact that Apaches, renegades in general, set great store by saving face. Jeff smoked and soaked, and lathered up after awhile, then used his hat to sluice off with when he stood up, and came to the conclusion that by gawd his partner was probably right. That lousy mule-stealing rag-head and his mangy grass-seed-eaters were waiting up the river.

By the time Jeff had dried off on the soggy towel, which had still been a little mouldy before Ben had used it, and then flung it on the slivery old wooden floor exactly as he had prohibited Ben from doing, while he then slowly got dressed, the sun was nearing its midday zenith. Outside, there were no shadows, just sunlight.

Jeff walked out, tipped down his hat to protect his eyes, and paused to turn from habit, perhaps, to look for dust off to the east. There was none, of course.

But when he walked forward to the roadway he saw a dusty top-buggy with a sweat-streaked harness-horse between the shafts standing in hot sunshine, and it annoyed him that anyone would deliberately tie their sweaty horse where he was sure to be galled by the sunlight. It did not occur to him that the rig had come a very great distance at a fast gait for a reason, until he sauntered around the side of the café-building and saw three men slouching in over-hang shade smoking, talking softly back and forth, and something in the back of his head rang a bell. He had never in his life seen Lem Steele. He did not even know now which of the three buggy-passengers was Steele, but instinct told him as distinctly as possible where that top-buggy had come from and who owned it. As he stepped up on to the plankwalk behind the three hard-looking strangers with their tied-down guns he drew and cocked his Colt and said, "You know, gents, only a real son of a bitch would use a horse that hard, then tie him out where the salt-sweat and the sunshine will make blisters on his back and neck and sides." He smiled. "Shuck the guns, then you there with the grey hair, you take that horse and rig across and tie him in the shade over in front of the jailhouse. And you other two bastards—you just look like you don't like what I'm doing and I'll salt you down for keeps."

Ben and Drake Haslett were leading their horses, plus a third saddled animal, from the liverybarn into the yard out front and saw what was happening up in front of the café. They stared in complete astonishment, then Ben did not even hesitate, he handed the reins of Jeff's horse to the lawman and started walking northward up the roadway leading his own horse. He drew his gun as he walked.

Drake Haslett looked and sputtered, and swore aloud, then also started walking up the roadway, but he had to put both sets of reins in the same hand before he could also draw. But Drake drew to prevent trouble, if he could. He had nothing else in mind as he glowered at the men up in front of the café. His glare included Jeff Hill.

13

TROUBLE AT LINCOLN!

The trio of strangers seemed dumbfounded and they had a right to feel that way. They had been standing there talking, with no inkling the disreputable-looking individual who emerged from around behind them had even looked in their direction, and a moment later he had a cocked sixgun aimed at them and was giving orders.

He was serious. They had little doubt of that when he addressed them, but when they stood staring and saw his finger tightening round the trigger they decided he was as crazy as a coot, and moved with extreme caution to obey his injunction about shedding their guns.

Two other men were coming up the roadway. They also had drawn guns. To the strangers it seemed they had either walked into some kind of trap, some kind of deadly involvement, or perhaps the approaching armed men were going to neutralize the crazy man. In either case they stood looking at Jeff as though uncertain about their course of action—then the man

with the grey around his ears, standing in the fore-
front, saw that finger curling and said, "All right,
partner, all right. I'll go lead the horse across the
road. Just relax. Just slack off a little and everything'll
be fine."

Jeff said, "First the guns. Dump 'em!"

The greying man muttered to his youthful, bitter-
eyed companions and all three men lifted away their
Colts and let them fall.

The greying man smiled at Jeff. "Now I'll care for
the horse. You're plumb right, we should have tied
him across in the shade." He stepped slowly to the
edge of the plankwalk, then moved down into the
roadway, went over to untie the horse, and looked
stealthily over his shoulder.

Jeff had moved. He now was directly behind the
other two strangers. He saw the greying-man's glance
and waited for whatever it portended to happen, but
apparently being disarmed made a lot of difference
because the greying man simply loosened the rope,
turned the horse and started across the road, leading
the animal, which was in turn pulling the dusty top-
buggy.

Ben was fifty yards southward. Drake Haslett was
almost that far behind Ben Hurley back down in the
direction of the liverybarn. Elsewhere, a few astonished pedestrians had seen the gun in Jeff Hill's fist
and had ducked clear, then had poked heads from
such places as the barber shop, the general store, and
over across the road from the stores on that side too,
but generally, probably because there had been no
noisy altercation, the majority of townsmen were going serenely about their affairs up and down the
roadway with no inkling.

The pair of disarmed men, with Jeff behind them,

were bitterly looking over where their companion was retying the buggy-animal in shade. Jeff shoved his gunbarrel into a soft back and said, "Is that Lem Steele over yonder?"

Now, it began to be clear to the strangers that the man with the sixgun was not a madman. One of them cleared his throat and glanced at his companion. Jeff cruelly rammed the gun into the man's back, hard. The stranger gasped and tried to ease away but Jeff remained close to him and repeated the question.

"Is that Sheriff Steele from Verde Wells?"

The stranger's reply was in a husky tone of voice. "That's Lem Steele, only he ain't a sheriff, he's a town marshal over at Verde Wells."

Jeff let the man know the gun was still back there. "What's he doing over here?"

The stranger did not answer. He did not have to. Across the road the greying man yelled to his friends to jump clear. The greying man accompanied that outcry with a sudden swift movement which allowed him to duck under the horse's neck and emerge upon the far side of the beast. He then took several long steps to reach the far side of the top-buggy where he could peek out and see without being seen. He had a gun in his hand. He may have got it from inside the buggy or he may have had a second weapon in another holster, but as he leaned to aim and called again for his friends to duck clear, he fired and the man in front of Jeff was already dropping over into a low crouch. The bullet shattered the barber-shop window, missing both Jeff and the man in front of him by about twelve inches. From the barber shop someone let out a great squawk.

Ben Hurley ran to the east-side plankwalk, gun up and riding lightly in his right hand. He could not see the man on the far side of the rig but he knew where he was.

Drake yelled for the shooting to stop, and it hadn't even started. He also ran to the east side of the road, abandoning the horses he'd been leading exactly as Ben Hurley had done. The animals stood uncertainly for a moment, then turned back, and someone captured them down near the liverybarn before they could break over into a belly-down run and leave town by the southern coach-road.

Jeff held his fire. The pair of strangers in front of him were twisting first one way then another way, afraid to obey the order to flee and afraid to remain where they were. Jeff told them not to move, and with an outstretched arm grabbed the farthest man and shoved him closer to his companion. This formed a better protection for Jeff.

Ben yelled to the man on the far side of the wagon. "Pitch away the gun, mister. You're cut off on all sides. Pitch it away!"

There was no sound nor movement from the far side of the buggy. Evidently Lem Steele believed he could still gun his way out of trouble.

Then Drake Haslett, star in place on his shirt, walked past Ben, gun cocked and low-held, got almost to the tethered buggy-horse and called for the stranger to drop his gun. Maybe the man could see Drake and maybe not, but in either case he seemed about to raise his hand to fire again towards Jeff when a man wearing a greasy brown apron stepped from a shop northward of the buggy with a sawed-off shotgun in both hands. The legend on the window behind this newcomer to the fracas said simply: 'Gunsmith.'

That scattergun would have cut the greying man in

two, and it would also have shredded the near side of the top-buggy.

The lanky, shock-headed leathery-skinned individual holding the shotgun said, "Throw down that pistol you son of a bitch!" He raised his shotgun a degree aiming it squarely for Lem Steele's middle.

Steele looked half around without moving anything but his head, saw the scattergun, saw the look in the face of the man holding it in the gunshop doorway, eased off the hammer of his Colt and let it fall.

The gunsmith raised his voice a notch but did not take his eyes off Lem Steele. "Hey, Drake; he's unarmed. Come and get him if you want him."

Haslett and Ben Hurley came along and over across the road. Jeff growled and shoved his pair of human shields off the plankwalk into the roadway to herd them over there also.

When he got close enough he said, "Ben; that there is Lem Steele, the man who was to come from Verde Wells and buy our mules from Talador." He accompanied that announcement by giving the other two men rough shoves forward. "These'll be his running-mates."

Drake went up and down Steele, then turned and without a word did the same to the other pair. One of them had a boot-knife and the other one had a derringer. Drake shook his head and glared as he gestured for the trio of strangers to head down to the jailhouse.

Ben put up his weapon, watched Haslett herding away the prisoners, and turned as Jeff said, "Now what—we still got to go up to the canvas-camp, don't we?"

Ben shrugged. "I never would have guessed Steele would have shown up over here. Let's go find out why. The ride to camp will have to wait a spell."

Now, finally, the town was alive with both spectators and the inevitable know-it-alls whose wild speculations would be months dying. None of them knew the facts yet, but that never seemed to deter people from creating what they thought might be the facts, outlandish as those were in many instances. But when Ben and Jeff went to the jailhouse, of all those garrulous onlookers, none had dredged up the courage to walk into the sheriff's office, which indicated that they were not always incorrect in their judgments; they knew what a disagreeable temper Drake Haslett had when he was aroused.

Drake had already locked up the companions of the Verde Wells lawman. Their hats and weapons were atop his desk. The hats were up-ended and full of the private property from the pockets of the men down in the cell-room. The third hat, along with the personal things of Lem Steele, was sitting directly in front of Drake, who was going over them one at a time under the baleful look of the man with greying temples across the desk from him.

As the pair of freighters walked in Steele was speaking in a low, uncompromising tone. "You couldn't hold me nor my hired hands even if you had a warrant, Sheriff, because all we did was drive over here from Verde Wells, and run into a crazy-man in front of the tonsorial parlour. You don't have a charge against any of us."

Ben came through the doorway, listened a moment, then said, "Drake; you need a charge?"

Haslett raised untroubled eyes from his examination of the wallet in his hand, and said, "Hell no. Since when do I need a charge to lock someone up?" He then went back to completing his inspection of the wallet, and when he'd finished he tossed it atop the other things in the hat, reared back in his chair and with thumbs hooked, put a sceptical look at Lem Steele. "You had ought to have been smarter," he said, "than to leave Verde Wells. Steele, I got some old warrants for you that go back five, six years."

"Outdated," exclaimed the greying man. "The statute of limitations ran out on 'em long ago."

Drake considered, scratched lightly, then said, "What's a statue of limitations?"

"Stat*ute* of limitations!"

"All right. What is a stat*ute* of limitations?"

Steele stared, then turned slowly and eyed the pair of men leaning against the front wall over by the doorway. When he faced forward again he said, "You got no decent charge. That feller over by the door threw down on us with no cause at all. Said something about abuse of animals and made me go take my buggy-horse across the road in the shade so's his back wouldn't get galled . . . I figured he was a madman, a *pukutsi*. Some kind of crazy feller, so when I got across the road I tried to free my friends and shoot that bunch-quitter . . . Now where is the crime in that?"

Drake smiled coolly. "Steele, you're talkin' through your hat. What I want to hear from you is why you came over here today."

"You got a town ordinance over here that says folks can't visit?" demanded the greying man, his malevolent eyes boring into Drake Haslett. "You haul in every stranger who arrives in Lincoln and . . . ?"

"Just answer my question," said Haslett, and when the greying man seemed unwilling to obey, Drake leaned forward, shot up to his feet and lost all semblance of amiability as he gestured. "All right, we'll do it your way. On your feet. I'll lock you up and throw away the key like I did with your friends. I said —on your feet!"

Lem Steele rose slowly. Even without a gun in his hip-holster or in his shoulder-holster, he looked menacing. Jeff and Ben were even more interested in him than Drake was. Their concern went back to a suspected tie-in with the rag-head raiders. It was in their view more than just a suspected affiliation.

Ben said, "Steele. You know a man named Hank Armstrong?"

The renegade turned coldly. He studied Ben, then Jeff, before answering. "Yeah; he's the law over at Gila. *Was* the law over there anyway."

"He was also our prisoner until last night," stated Ben. "He filled in a lot of blank spaces for us. About Talador, about you, about how the raiders do business through you. How you would have bought our mules, which Talador ran off and delivered to a box-canyon over there for you to drive out and look at."

Steele curled his lip. "You believe Armstrong? Hell! anyone around Verde Wells or Gila knows Hank Armstrong would lie when the truth would fit better."

"Then you don't have any tie-in with Talador?" said Ben, and watched Steele's face closely, and when the renegade lawman hung fire about answering, Ben said, "Go ahead and answer. I want to hear you deny it."

Steele turned very cautious. "Why?" he said. "What can you make out of a denial?"

"That you're a liar by the clock," retorted Ben. "Go ahead and deny it."

Instead, Steele turned, walked to the cell-room door and silently waited until Drake unlocked the door, then Steele walked through with one final, and contemptuous, glance over his shoulder.

Ben let his breath out noisily and faced Jeff. "It was a bluff and he out-bluffed me."

"Wasn't any bluff," argued Jeff. "We know darned well he's tied in with the rag-heads."

"Can't prove it though," stated Ben, and turned as Sheriff Haslett came back into the room, turned to lock the cell-room door, and said, "You can't get talk out of a man like that just by standin' and arguing with him." Drake straightened up and dropped the brass key into a pocket. "You got to take them into one of the cells, close the door, and punch hell out of them. You'd be surprised how that'll jar a feller's memory."

Ben and Jeff would not have been the least bit surprised, but Ben started rolling a smoke and Jeff took up the conversation with a question.

"How long can you hold him, Drake?"

Haslett was nonchalant about that. "Like I said before—a hundred times—you give me a real good reason to lock someone into one of the cells, and by gawd he can stay there until summer arrives for all I care."

"Is that legal?"

Drake looked pained as he crossed to the desk and swept those hats containing the personal effects of his prisoners into a deep drawer, then said, "It must be legal, for gosh sakes, I'm a lawman and I do it right straight along."

He finished at the desk and put a quizzical look upon Jeff. "How the hell did you know that feller was Lem Steele?"

Jeff's reply was candid. "I didn't. I thought he might be, so I stepped in behind them and when I got the

chance shoved a gun into the back of that thin-faced
one and he told me which of them was Steele. And
five seconds later all hell busted loose."

Ben turned, opened the door, looked up and down
the roadway and stepped forth. "They got our horses
tied out front down at the liverybarn. Let's ride out to
the canvas-camp and get that over with. Then we can
come back, eat a decent supper, put on some clean
clothes, get shaved and sleep the lousy clock around."

They all three left the jailhouse and Drake turned
back to lock the front door. Jeff said, "Why lock it,
those fellers can't get out of the cells."

"You simpleton," muttered Drake Haslett, turning
to lead off southward. "I don't worry about folks
getting *out* of my jailhouse. I worry about their friends
going *in* while I'm gone, and busting them out."

Jeff said, "Oh. I never thought of that," and hiked
along with the other two.

14

UP THE RIVER!

The same thought was in each mind as the three of them left town on their way over to the riverbank, where they would follow the road over there leading northward, and the best explanation Jeff could offer had to do with Steele's need for seventeen head of good mules.

Ben conceded this, but offered the opinion that since their mules were not the only ones around, and in fact once they had retrieved their mules smart thieves would not make a second attempt to steal them—although those same thieves, at least the Apache thieves, would want to redeem their "honour" —the real reason for Lem Steele to come to Lincoln had to do with something else.

Drake scowled. "What else? If you think he figured to rob us over here—we don't have a bank and the general store sends out money for the merchants every three days on the stages, so what would he get?"

It was possible, too, that Steele had not arrived in Lincoln for any of the reasons the horsemen had thus

far discussed. They were a mile from town over
alongside the river when Ben came up with a fresh
suggestion. "He came over with his partners to have a
look at the men who stole mules right out from under
Talador's nose, so's he could maybe get us to throw in
with him and go into the raiding business."

Drake looked too disgusted to comment and Jeff
acted as though he hadn't heard right. "Why in hell
would anyone need another band of raiders?" demanded Jeff. "There are already five times as many of those
worthless bastards as there'd ought to be."

Ben threw up his arms. "What, then?" he demanded.
"And don't tell me again he had to have our mules
because there are plenty of mules around as good and
maybe even better than our mules."

Drake noticed how Ben did not stop looking up and
down the river as they were riding northward, and
eventually he said, "Ben; what the hell are you looking
for across the river? You act like an old cow that's lost
her calf."

Ben gave no reply but he stopped being so obvious
about the way he studied the opposite riverbank. He
even made a cigarette for which he felt absolutely no
need, lit it and offered the "makings" to Haslett, who
refused them and who instead dug around until he
found one of those long, thin, very crooked and very
strong Mexican cigars, which he lighted under the
close study of both his companions. Drake lit the thing
with the flourish of a man to whom cigars were a
distinct luxury.

Ben said, "I always figured cigars were what they
gave folks as they led them up the steps to a gallows,
or maybe when they walked them out to a stone wall
and left them out there."

Haslett looked at Ben with obvious distaste. "That's

the trouble with fellers like the pair of you," he said, and probably would have said more since he hadn't really said enough for it to be self-explanatory, when Jeff interrupted to say that cigars were a bad omen to him, and this annoyed the sheriff so much he turned against his latest detractor.

"Superstition," he exclaimed. "There's nothing worse in this world than ignorant folks and their superstitions!"

Ben suddenly yelled and dived off his horse, dragging the carbine from the saddle-boot with him. Jeff looked up, swung to peer across the river, then did the same, and while Drake Haslett was sitting up there eyes popped wide, cigar hanging slack as complete bewilderment took over, a ragged burst of abrupt gunfire erupted from across the river and northward where the willows were thickest.

Drake Haslett's horse dropped like a stone. He was dead before he hit the ground with all four legs tucked up. The sheriff flung free, kicked both feet out of the stirrups and catapulted himself over upon the left side of the horse where he landed in a heap, and had the hat rammed down on to his ears as he tried to prevent his momentum from carrying him far from the dead animal.

Ben was in some tules and willow-shoots along the bank of the river, invisible to the raiders across the water but not protected at all from lead as he crab-crawled closer to the water hoping for a chance to part the rushes and see across.

Jeff bolted. He did not turn towards the river, he turned away from it trying with all his might to make it into some spindly trees which were a few hundred yards south of the canvas-camp, and it was Jeff the raiders across the river were whooping and firing at.

Each time he would jump and land down running
with a fresh spurt of speed, the raiders would whoop
anew and try harder than ever to bring him down.
Their aim was not very exceptional, but in fairness the
distance was fair for carbines and the target was not
trying to hold to a direct course, he was sashaying
back and forth and pumping with both arms as he fled.
He had abandoned his Winchester after the first
couple of slugs spurted dust beneath his feet.

Haslett was allowed time to get prepared and to
push and wrench the jammed-down hat back up where
it was supposed to be.

Ben got down to the mud, to the last row of weeds
and jungle-like undergrowth, got his saddlegun pushed
ahead gently and finally could lie flat in the mud so
that when an Indian arose recklessly to take long aim
at Jeff, Ben shot him out of the rushes. The man
pushed himself back into half a sitting posture and
stared with disbelief, then he collapsed and behind
him someone made a trilling high call of warning.

The raiders turned in this new direction. From
around the head and neck of his dead horse Drake
Haslett, who was an excellent gunshot, took plenty of
time, fired, and must have dusted someone across the
Mescal because a man's sharp little yip of astonishment erupted in the wake of the gunshot.

Ben turned. "I told you," he yelled to Drake. "I told
you folks only smoke those damned things on their
way to the wall or the scaffold."

Haslett's cigar was broken in the middle but as yet
he had not realized it. Now, he chomped down harder
and yelled back. "You knew those bastards was over
there, damn you Ben Hurley! That's why you kept
looking over there, and that's how come you to yell and
dive off your horse!"

Someone among the opposite undergrowth had been tracking Drake by his voice and now dumped a bullet into his 'barricade'. It made a ripping, meaty sound and Drake abruptly went silent.

Ben looked around. Jeff had made it into the yonder trees. Ben shook his head. No one in his right mind would try to make that kind of a flight; no one in his right mind had any business believing he could outrun a bullet—even one fired by such traditionally bad marksmen as Apaches.

Several of those invisible raiders began to move, to shift position. Clearly, they had chosen the best ambushing site on their side of the Mescal, but since the ambush hadn't worked they were now becoming restless in their rushes and willows. They had never learned how to be stationary warriors. Ben caught a fleeting view now and then, of dark men moving quickly.

This actually was an Apache type conflict, and they were good at it providing they were left to their own tactics and strategy. Ben worried. He guessed that was Talador over yonder, and from what he had been told Talador had six men with him. Those were not insurmountable odds, unless all seven of those raiders went in different directions, and at least three of them came across to Ben's side of the river, which they could accomplish providing they went either up-river or down-river until they were safely out of sight, then swam or waded across and got into the underbrush on Ben's side—then the entire escapade could take a totally different turn.

Ben looked back at the dead horse. "Watch down-river," he called, mindful that Talador and his men could hear, and could probably also understand, what he said.

The answer was brusque and unfriendly. "You louse, Hurley! You could have told me back in town!"

"How could I have told you back in town when I wasn't sure of it myself!"

"You knew—well—you suspected!"

Ben sighed, looked up in the trees where his partner had gone, and decided to move away from this place a short distance. He inevitably wiggled the tules as he crawled very carefully, and across the river a *sabe* raider bracketed him, one shot ahead, one behind, and when the shot came for the middle, Ben had anticipated it and had rolled heavily down into the deeper mud. The third slug tore willows and rushes where Ben should have been.

He eased up a little and reached with his left hand to part the willows and peer out. He was coldly angry. But evidently that *coyotero* was as proficient at hiding as he was at bracketing a target. Ben saw nothing. He lay a long time waiting and still saw nothing, so in the end he crawled back up out of the mud.

The raiders were leaving. That became clear when Jeff finally got into the fight and systematically raked their hiding-place across the river with six bullets properly spaced and drilled in low and fast. Then he had to pause to reload and Ben wondered about that; wondered whether Jeff had more carbine cartridges.

He did have, because he opened up again, cutting willows and rushes and knocking bark from creek-willows which were also upon the opposite bank, and not a single raider fired back nor yelped nor exposed himself as he sought a safer place.

Ben crawled back up the bank and flattened where the dry ground was sun-warmed and the cover was adequate. He guessed that Talador would prefer going up the river to going down it closer to Lincoln.

Eventually he raised up and looked out, then dropped flat instantly. He drew no fire, but he got a caustic comment from Sheriff Haslett.

"You might as well let them shoot at your head. That's probably the part of your carcass a bullet can't do any damage to!"

Ben fished out his bandanna to dry mud and moisture from his hands as he called back. "Listen to me— suppose I hadn't insisted that you come up here with us today? Suppose you'd driven up here this evening with Miss Sansouci?"

"*Mrs.* Sansouci!"

"And those rag-head bastards had bushwhacked you?"

For a long time there was no answer, but eventually the lawman said, "Where are they?" in a different tone of voice.

"Gone," replied Ben. "I guess up-river to cross over and come down here and swarm all over us like a nest of hornets."

For a while the sheriff was silent and motionless, then he eventually did the same thing Ben had done, he raised up, dropped flat and waited. When there was no gunfire he tried that again, and the second time he remained raised up a little longer, looking along the opposite riverbank. That time as he eased back down he echoed Ben's suspicion.

"Not a soul over there."

Ben's retort was tart. "I already told you that. You want to squat here until they're all around us, or do you want to get up yonder into the trees with Jeff and palaver?"

Haslett said, "Lead the way," and Ben replied to that using the same tart tone of voice. "You're sure as hell real hero material."

He did not waste time reconnoitring. This time he sprang to his feet and raced for it. Behind him the sheriff did likewise, but the sheriff was nowhere nearly as good a sprinter. He lost ground steadily and when Ben burst past the initial stand of trees the sheriff was still lumbering along swinging his carbine as though it were a wand.

Jeff laughed as he watched, and when Ben rushed towards him the taller freighter stepped from behind a tree and made a sweeping salutation with his disreputable old hat. Ben stopped and leaned on a tree breathing hard.

"You see 'em?" he panted.

Jeff pointed northward. "They trickled up the river one at a time. There were only six of them."

"That's all there were supposed to be."

"No damn it," responded Jeff annoyedly. "There are supposed to be seven. Talador and six raiders. I think when you and that feller to the south of their bushwhack duelled when we first rode up, you nailed that one. That would account for there being only six."

This brief discussion was interrupted by Sheriff Haslett's belated arrival. Jeff turned and without any expression, said, "I was clean-shaven when you left that brush-clump down yonder."

Drake had a retort but he was panting too hard to waste the breath. They explained to him where the raiders were and he simply bobbed his head and leaned there sucking air. Finally, when he was able to speak, he said, "We'd ought to find the horses and head for town for help."

Jeff disagreed. "You'd ought to give up those Mex cigars, Drake," he said, then changed the subject with a suggestion. "What we'd ought to do is head right on up through the canvas-camp and do it fast, and set up

an ambush, and shoot the butts off those mule-stealin'
whelps as they come slippin' down here to try and
bushwhack us . . . Ben?"

They did not hold the council in the trees it had
seemed they might hold. Ben scotched it by respond-
ing to his partner's suggestion without commenting but
by hoisting his carbine and starting off northward up
through the trees, and he looked worse now than he
had looked when they had first arrived back in
Lincoln. He had been wallowing in rank mud, in tules
and rushes, and even his hat looked indescribably
filthy as he led off.

Drake Haslett followed, still breathing hard, and
once when Jeff turned from their swift passage up
towards the canvas-camp and started to speak, Drake
glowered and said, "Mind your own darned business.
It's not the Mex stogies anyway, it's just that I haven't
been exercisin' much lately. Otherwise I'd have more
wind than both of you put together!"

Jeff nodded. "Hot air anyway," he murmured, and
resumed trotting in Ben's wake.

They came through the trees to the clearing which
surrounded the place where they had made their
camp. As nearly as they could determine from just
looking out there, the camp had not been ransacked,
but Ben turned off in the direction of the river and
without hesitation burst forth into the open country
and zigzagged through the green willows and undergrowth as he bypassed the camp.

Their huge old Missouri wagon stood in brilliant
sunshine like some scarred and ancient behemoth.
They were tempted to climb into it and use it as a
fort, but in the end Ben negated that with a shrewd
comment.

"That's exactly where they'll figure we are."

He led them closer to the river until they were forced to slow to a slogging walk because of the muddy terrain and also because the undergrowth down through there turned more tangled and primeval. It was the first decent cover they'd had since abandoning the trees farther back, and up westerly from the riverbank.

From here on Ben was as watchful as he'd been when they'd first arrived up in this area. Drake Haslett, watching Hurley, decided privately that Ben was probably the best of them for taking the lead and although he still harboured resentment over what he felt positive had been a deliberate scheme to get him up here in a fight with raiders, he was fair. Ben made an excellent scout.

One certain indication that they were not alone up through the tules hereabouts was the total absence of birdsong. Usually this time of year the riverbank would have been full of nesting, fighting, arguing, food-hunting birds. This morning that had been true, this afternoon it was not true at all. There was not a sound anywhere around.

15

A FREIGHTER'S TACTICS

Ben stopped finally where the covert was as good as it was going to get farther along, and hunkered down. Jeff and the lawman came along to also drop down out of sight in the rank growth at riverside. They were a hundred yards north of the canvas-camp and while Ben thought they could probably get another fifty yards northward, he also said where they now were, they would be unseen, and if they took a long chance to get up farther, they might lose their entire advantage if the raiders were also moving swiftly.

"Or out of the country," suggested Haslett, and got a pair of pitying looks before Jeff said, "We made 'em look very bad. They got to correct that."

"And the mules," Ben put in.

Drake scowled. "What mules?"

"The ones we deliberately left back in town," explained Ben Hurley, "but they don't know that yet, do they?"

Drake picked out one word. "*Deliberately* left back in town?"

Ben sighed. He hadn't meant to say it that way.

An owl hooted, mournfully, and from farther inland a jaybird scolded so realistically the listening men down by the river marvelled. Drake Haslett gestured. "They're stalkin' down to the area around the wagon." He acted as though he were prepared to seize the initiative and go Apache-hunting. Ben growled at him. "Just set and wait."

"I thought you said we'd ambush 'em?" snarled the resentful lawman.

Ben nodded. "That's exactly what we're going to do. Now just set and wait."

Haslett was not a man who took orders with any grace. "Wait for what?"

Again that mournful owl called, and this time he was much closer and coming down along the edge of the river. Ben and Jeff stared at Haslett. The sheriff reddened slightly and looked away.

The jaybird-caller did not make his unique announcement of personal location again for a long time. By the time he was close enough to the old Missouri wagon to sound off, Ben and Jeff and Drake were crouching like three coiled rattlesnakes listening to the stealthy approach of someone between them and the river.

It was the 'owl' of course, but what the ambushers were most interested in was whether the 'owl' was alone or not. They had no way of making that determination without also risking noise, so they waited and listened, and scarcely breathed until the raider was close enough for them to detect the sound of his carbine being bumped along either behind him or at his side.

Jeff gently lay aside his Winchester, shed his old

hat, ignored the look of his partner and the sheriff and eased westerly down through the rushes as silently as a snake. He and the raider were on a collision course, but without the raider having any idea this was so.

There was a moment of utter stillness as though the raider had detected something, had suddenly turned fearful and wary, then the 'owl' hooted again and on the last note Jeff rose up ten feet to one side, saw the man with both hands cupped to his lips, and sailed over the undergrowth to land squarely atop the most astonished Indian in all Creation. In fact the Apache still held his hands cupped to his face when his black eyes bulged in surprise at the soaring adversary dropping towards him from the sky.

Ben and Drake arose, guns cocked in case there were more than one, but evidently the 'owl' had been making his sortie alone, because as he and Jeff threshed and kicked and arched and grunted in mortal combat among the bullrushes, no other raiders sprang forward to take a hand in the fight.

The Indian was smaller than Jeff but heavier and much more compactly thick. He was as strong as an ox. His main disadvantage was that although he tried repeatedly to club Jeff over the head with a meaty fist, he actually had no knowledge of how to fight at such close quarters without either a knife or gun or hatchet, and Jeff made very certain he did not have an opportunity to get at the gun round his middle or the carbine he'd brought along. If the man had a belt-knife—and it was almost a certainty that he did have —Jeff did not see it and the Indian was unable to reach it.

Twice, Jeff hooked him hard under the chin and both times although the raider dropped his head and pushed in against his adversary he did not slacken up in his desperate clawing and striking, so evidently he had a jaw of iron.

Next, Jeff tried to push the man back far enough to belt him in the face, between the eyes or across the bridge of the nose, and both times he made this effort the Apache, who had a neck as thick as a stone column, resisted successfully.

Ben came over, gunbarrel poised as a club, but the Indian saw this fresh danger, gripped Jeff round the middle and hurled him bodily sidewards then rolled away with him. Ben swore and jumped ahead but the pair of fighting men were hopelessly intertwined and moving.

It was Drake Haslett who sprang across the straining bodies, caught the Indian by his coarse hair and using all his strength drew the man's head steadily back. Then Drake pressed the barrel of his cocked Colt into the man's throat.

The Apache's muddy eyes looked directly up into Haslett's face. Drake said in Spanish, "That is enough!"

The Indian gradually loosened his grip on Jeff, gradually allowed Jeff to free himself.

Without a word Drake yanked the Indian's head forward by the hair, released his grip and swung the pistol. The Indian had thick hair and evidently he also had a thick skull because Drake's gunbarrel bounced back as the Apache drooped all over and sprawled lifelessly to one side, unconscious but evidently not hurt because there was not even a break in his scalp despite the force of the blow.

Jeff sat up breathing hard. He looked around, looked back and said, "Much obliged, Sheriff. That's one I wouldn't want to have to fight more than maybe once a week." He got his old hat from Ben, along with his carbine, and Ben did not allow either of them any time for additional talk or rest, he jerked his head and called on them to follow after, then he started northward very briskly up the riverbank.

They followed, Jeff breathing hard but gamely keeping up until they were a quarter mile onward and Ben stepped down into the river heading across, then Jeff hissed at his partner.

"What the hell do you think you're doing? They'll be in our camp by now, south of here, and not expectin' us to come in behind them."

Ben kept on wading. The river was shallow enough here so that water scarcely reached above their knees. Ben turned to make certain they were following, and held both his weapons overhead as he said, "Keep up and don't stop. I don't figure they'll see us but if they do, and we're out here like three darned sitting ducks. . . ."

"You're running from them," Drake said accusingly. "By gawd I'd never have believed it, Ben."

"Oh shut up, will you," growled their leader. "We're not running from anyone."

"No; then just what the hell are we doing?" Drake demanded.

"We're going after six head of horses, that's what we're doing," snapped Ben, and waded harder than ever when he was in mid-stream where the full force of the river's sluggish current sucked at their feet and legs in an effort to either up-end them or slow them down.

By the time they reached the opposite shore Ben was breathing hard. Jeff, who hadn't begun this latest odyssey in too good a shape, dropped belly-down in the mud and willows and did not move as Drake

.Haslett stepped over him and proceeded another few yards before halting and looking back.

There was no movement back on the west side of the river and no indication that they had been discovered. Ben leaned on his carbine and caught his breath, then said, "Get up, Jeff. That's all you been doin' lately—resting."

Jeff struggled upright and Ben turned southward down through the trees and willows. The cover over on the Mescal's eastern bank was superior to the cover on the opposite shoreline.

Drake waited for Jeff but Ben did not even glance back and his stride was almost as quick and springy as before. He had no clear idea where the raiders left their horses but he was confident of one thing. Wherever those animals had been tied, there was no one guarding them. Talador had six riders with him. Originally there had been seven men in the ambush over on this side of the river, which meant of course that the horses did not have a sentinel with them, and if this may have seemed reckless to those who in later days would go over the details of this skirmish, it actually was not reckless at all—until Talador had led his men across the river, then it had become reckless because Talador had allowed his horses to be on the wrong side of the Mescal, but neither he nor his men would have thought this was so for a very good reason. When they crossed over to carry the initiative to the freighters they firmly believed they were only facing a couple of men, and that they had driven those two men either to flight or on to the defensive.

Maybe they would have been correct, too, if their adversaries had been different individuals.

Ben Hurley had to range back and forth to the east of the place where the raiders had first tried their ambush. He knew the horses would be farther back from the river, but exactly how far back, or where, precisely, he had no idea and therefore his zigzagging course, tiring as it became to the men following him, was his best way to locate the tethered animals. He was also aware of something else. Talador was shrewd and clever; it would only take him a few moments to divine what had happened once he became convinced the freighters were not down in the area of their canvas-camp.

When Talador realized what Ben was up to, he was going to come charging back across the river in a desperate rush to reach his saddle-stock before the *pind-o-lick-o-yees* found them.

Ben did not believe Talador could accomplish this, but as time passed without the horses appearing in among the easterly undergrowth his confidence dwindled. Then Drake said, "We got to split up otherwise those damned rag-heads'll be coming back over here before we get lucky."

It was sound strategy and that is what they did. Less than two or three minutes later Jeff sang out. He had trotted due easterly out into a clearing which was completely surrounded by creek-willows, and there were not six tethered horses, but seven of them, and a particular large and powerful spotted horse, sorrel and white, with glass eyes, was adorned in a magnificently silver-mounted *charro* saddle. That, Jeff guessed on the spur of the moment, would be Talador's personal mount.

Jeff turned as Ben appeared from the south and Drake came hurrying ahead from the north. Without a word they hastened over and freed all seven horses. Jeff appropriated the big spotted horse, vaulted into the elegant Mexican saddle—found the stirrups a foot too short—and reined around to help his companions as they also got astride and hazed the remaining horses easterly out through the riverbank undergrowth in a reckless rush.

They were a half-mile out over the open country eastward when several gunshots erupted far back. Their response was to push the driven saddle-stock faster, and to eventually swing southward with them down in the direction of Lincoln.

Ben caught his hat as it almost took to the air and crushed it furiously down over his ears. Drake had straddled a small Mexican horse with a fine Barb head and a stout heart. The little horse would not be outrun by any of them not even the big spotted horse as they raced along well beyond gun-range of those screaming and gesticulating raiders back on the edge of the clearing where the horses had been tied.

It was Jeff's idea to recross the river, and as he gestured in that direction he told Ben and Drake unless they could find their own loose-stock there was a fair chance the Indians might find them and escape. At least two of the Indians might escape on their two horses.

They splashed back to the west side of the Mescal, and sashayed back and forth in search of their private mounts but found neither hide nor hair. Drake was sardonic about this. His dead animal, he said, would have headed for the liverybarn in town sure as night followed day, because he was barn-sour in the first place, and in the second place he had done this before —a couple of times when he'd managed to untie himself, something which had taught Drake Haslett to cordially despise that animal. For that reason he wasn't sorry the horse was dead.

They had to assume that the other two horses might

do the same thing, head back towards town, and turned in that direction themselves.

The day was dying. It had been working along towards that inevitable fate for some time but without anyone up near the freight-camp being especially aware of it. Now, as the trio of muddy, rumpled and agitated horsemen riding their Apache horses and driving more Apache horses ahead of them, swept along towards town, the shadows seemed to want to help in concealing them.

The sun was no longer over in the west although this time of year daylight would continue for several hours on towards nightfall, and when dusk arrived it would be so belated that at best it could only linger for about an hour before darkness came.

They had Lincoln in sight, finally, before it began to appear that they would be unable to reach the place until darkness had finally settled. They had to slack off and rest their mounts. They also had to make some adjustments which they hadn't had the time to make earlier. Those square, steel Mexican stirrups, for example, on the saddle under Jeff, were flopping with painful results. He hauled down to a walk and adjusted both stirrup-leathers, first one then the other, as the horse walked steadily along. When he was able finally to use the stirrups the *esilla charro* proved to be much more comfortable than it had been before.

As he settled back and looked around, his partner turned towards Sheriff Haslett to say, "You could get in touch with the army. They shouldn't have too much trouble running down Talador and his rag-heads on foot."

Drake nodded. "First thing when we get back," he agreed, and smiled at Ben. "I owe you an apology. I guess I jumped to a conclusion. I guess you really didn't know those bastards would be up there waiting."

Ben lifted his hat, vigorously scratched, dropped the hat down and said, "I knew. Well; I sure as hell suspected they'd be up there. You were right when you figured that's why we didn't fetch along our mules."

"Why you lousy bastard," roared the sheriff, and Ben flapped his arms, unperturbed as he continued on down to the edge of town with Jeff grinning over at him.

16

ONE ANGRY COWMAN

The liveryman was out back when they arrived down
the far side of town and swung inward towards the
public corrals with their Indian horses. He stood leaning upon a manure-fork as though he would fall flat
without it, and stared. He had already survived one
brush with those two filthy-looking, unshaven freighters but now he stared hardest at Drake Haslett, who
did not look much more presentable than the villains
he was riding with.

The liveryman could have gone forth to open a
corral gate but he instead remained completely out of
it; allowed those murderous-looking individuals to
corral the horses by themselves.

Only when all three of them came striding towards
him in the heavy gloom did he straighten up off the
manure-fork.

"Feed 'em," growled Jeff. "And providing they'll let
you get that close—cuff 'em off too, and give them a
little grain." Jeff and Ben halted to look balefully at

the liveryman, who in turn put a questioning gaze upon the sheriff.

Drake nodded and turned, heading up in the direction of the jailhouse, and again the townsmen on both sides of the road, evening-strollers for the most part, scarcely noticed the sheriff nor the pair of disreputable-looking armed men walking soberly in his wake.

Sometimes it was possible for events to occur without anyone but the actual participants, and perhaps a handful of other people, having any idea untoward things had happened. It had been that way when Ben and Jeff had arrived back in Lincoln with their mules and it was that way again now, but this last time there was a better explanation. There was no moon yet and very few stars.

Drake lit the lamp on his desk, then went to the centre of the office to stand on a chair and lift down the ceiling-lantern to also light it. In all that orange glow, when he climbed off the chair and turned, Ben and Jeff looked even worse to him than they had looked to the stableman, but all he said was: "Fire up the stove and set that coffeepot atop it. I'll be back as soon as I've sent word by way of the stage company over to the commandant at Fort Meade. The sooner they get a detail scouring up the river the sooner they'll round up those raiders."

Jeff went to poke kindling into the stove while Ben rolled a cigarette and lit it while watching his partner's endeavours.

Someone grasped the latch from outside and poked a head in to stare at the pair of mud-caked, unsmiling men in the lighted sheriff's office, and without a word drew back, quietly closed the door and quickly departed.

"These damned people," complained Ben.

They got the coffeepot set atop the stove, got it full of water from a bucket nearby and when Ben turned Jeff was holding the copper ring with the brass key on it which unlocked the cell-room door. They exchanged a long look, and without speaking used the key to let themselves into the cell-room. It was both gloomy and stuffy in there. Ben lighted a lamp and hooked it from a ceiling hanger, and Jeff walked down to look in at the three men from Verde Wells.

One of the prisoners started to swear and complain, then he looked more closely at the pair of filthy apparitions in the corridor and seemed to lose his voice.

Ben reached under his coat and drew the sixgun hanging there. He smiled in at Lem Steele. "The sheriff's gone for a while," he said, still smiling. "You son of a bitch I'm going to splatter your head across the wall back yonder."

Ben raised the Colt and very slowly cocked it. The pair of younger prisoners were speechless and utterly still as they stared at Ben.

Lem Steele went white to the hairline. "Wait," he said hoarsely. "They'll hear you outside. The town'll come running and. . . ."

"The town," stated Jeff, "is plumb in favour of this. Before you go to hell, mister, maybe you'd like to know we set Talador and his raiders on foot a couple, three miles up the river and brought their horses down here and corralled them, and the sheriff has gone to set the army on those rag-heads before they can get very far on foot."

Ben stepped to the bars and started to push his sixgun through to take a rest on a cross-beam. Lem Steele had no place to go; his cell was only about fifteen feet square with nothing in it but a bunk bolted to the wall, a little stool, and a high, steel-barred little narrow window.

One of the younger men suddenly found his voice. "Hey, mister; wait a minute before you start shooting."

Ben said, "What for?" without taking his eyes off Lem Steele.

"Are you figuring on being the executioner of all three of us, maybe?"

Ben stepped back and turned to face the younger man. "One at a time," he said. "Steele first—you second."

"Well, mister," stated the younger man, his words and voice gaining strength as he spoke. "I can tell you a hell of a lot you never could guess about."

"Such as?" asked Ben, turning his cocked Colt on the younger man. "Who the hell are you?"

"Carl Ottinger," said the younger man. "I been working as deputy town marshal for Mister Steele over at. . . ."

"Where are you wanted?" growled Ben.

Ottinger's eyes jumped past Ben to Jeff, then back to Ben again. "That's what I was fixin' to tell you. Not about me, but there's at least ten wanted men over at Verde Wells and I can identify every one for you."

The other younger man in the cell with the speaker sat on the edge of a bunk smoking and sceptically looking upwards at the speaker. He did not seem to be indignant over what had just been said by his cellmate, but across the corridor in the cell where Lem Steele was locked in, the look was more than indignant, it was murderous as Steele said, "He's lyin' to you, mister, he couldn't point out a single wanted man over in Verde Wells. He's just sayin' all that to get on your side."

Ben turned towards Steele. "Sure he could. He could point you out."

"There's no warrant in force against me," exclaimed Steele.

"You lousy liar," replied Ben, and moved closer to the cell-bars. "You were going to buy our mules from Talador. You bought some horses belonging to an old man over here named Burns. You've been dealing in stolen livestock brought over into your private foot-hills since Hector was a pup, and if you deny it, Steele, we can bring in Hank Armstrong from Gila who'll testify that you've been doing it. Well . . . ?"

Steele looked from Ben's face to the cocked Colt. He looked past the Colt to Carl Ottinger across the corridor and his expression congealed into a look of lethal fury. He did not seem as fearful now as he had seemed ten minutes earlier, but neither did he seem willing to take chances.

When Ben repeated that "Well?" the Verde Wells lawman shrugged. Ben said, "That's no answer you bastard," so Lem Steele grumbled his retort without meeting Ben's stare.

"Yeah; I buy loose-stock."

"Out of those secret canyons you got gated off back up in the foothills?"

"Yeah."

"And you buy 'em from raiders like Talador?"

"Yeah."

"And you know they're stolen when you buy 'em?"

Steele raised sulphurous eyes. He and Ben exchanged a long look before Steele grudgingly said, "Yeah," again, in a tone so low Jeff had to strain to catch the word.

Ben eased off the dog of his sixgun and holstered the weapon. "When the sheriff gets back there'll be a warrant in force against you," he told the renegade lawman. "But I still believe the answer to men like you is a shooting. It saves time and work—and a lot of hard-earned taxpayers' money!"

He and Jeff returned to the office and the coffee was briskly boiling so they drew off a couple of cupfuls. It was the blackest, bitterest, strongest coffee Ben or Jeff had drunk in a 'coon's age. Neither of them finished it and Jeff removed the little pot from the stove.

Drake Haslett returned looking brisk and satisfied. As he went over to also draw off some coffee he said, "I got better'n I figured to get. There is an army patrol comin' south from a sashay on the cow ranges around Madisonville. The stage going north this evening will carry my message to their commanding officer telling him where Talador and his raiders are." Drake broadly smiled. "Our luck is changing, gents." He paused to wrinkle his nose. "You boys could go over and clean up if you wanted to. That riverbank mud don't smell real good."

Jeff was caustic. "If a man breathes through his mouth he can't smell, Sheriff, and in case you're interested Ben talked Lem Steele into admitting he buys stolen livestock from Talador, so that'll give you something to issue a warrant about, won't it?"

Ben sat down and fished around for his makings. While he was doing this the sheriff went to his desk and rummaged for one of those little cigars he'd been using lately. Jeff waited until he was ready to light the cigar then broke in with an earnest plea.

"Don't light that darned thing, Drake. Whatever you do don't fire another of those things up while I'm anywhere near. Look what you caused last time—

whole damned band of rag-head raiders liked to ambushed us, and. . . ."

"*What!*" yelled Drake Haslett. "What *I* caused! Damn you Jeff Hill! You and Ben! You both deliberately taken me up there and let me ride right down some lousy In'ian's rifle-barrel neat as a whistle! You could have got me killed and for all I know that's what you pair of rascals had in mind. Maybe so's you could get my job because you're fed up with freighting!"

Ben was comfortably smoking right up until Haslett made that last remark, then Ben was stung to life. He removed his cigarette to protest.

"I wouldn't have your lousy job for a wagon-load of high-grade ore, and freighting may be hard and dangerous but by gawd a man's his own boss, he don't have to polish no apples with a town council. And as for tryin' to lead you down some rag-head's rifle barrel. . . ."

Ben paused as a large cowman opened the roadside door and stamped in looking flintily towards the man over at the desk. The big cowman slammed the door, ignored Ben and Jeff and snarled at Sheriff Haslett.

"What the hell do folks pay you for, Drake, setting in here with a couple of unwashed tramps while the countryside is going to hell?"

Haslett sputtered as he reached to remove the cigar from his mouth before he could speak.

The big cowman sucked down a big breath and started in again. "A band of lousy rag-heads tried to stampede my saddle-horse remuda just before dark, by gawd, and they'd have succeeded too except that three of my riders was comin' in from the herd and saw them little bandy-legged bastards . . . And where is the law? Settin' in here on its bony butt smoking a greaser cigar and jawin' with some bums, that's where!"

This time it was Jeff who started to protest, and he had better luck than Drake had had. He walked over, tapped the large man's arm and when the cowman whirled Jeff said, "Wait a minute, mister, we're not tramps and he wasn't just settin' in here talking to us. My name is Hill and that's Ben Hurley my partner, and we're freighters."

Drake broke in. "Hey, hold it a minute Jeff." He turned towards the cowman. "Charley—you said some rag-heads tried to steal your remuda?"

"Yes, damn it, that's what I said, and I also said three of my cowboys was comin' to camp and saw them little devils and raised the yell to alert the rest of us."

Jeff and Ben were suddenly staring.

Drake Haslett said, "And—damn it let's have the rest of it, Charley!"

"We got all six of them. One of them made a hell of a battle of it. Had a sixgun in each hand." The large man shook his head as though in grudging admiration. "He was a fighter, I'll give him that."

"And you got him too?"

"Naw; we killed him," stated the rancher. "He's out front tied across a pack-mule."

"Where are the others?" asked Ben Hurley.

"Tied up," replied the cowman. "Tied up back to back and on their way to town in our camp-wagon. It was a hell of a running scrap for a while but those darned little devils was on foot or maybe they'd have got away in the dusk."

Drake sighed loudly. "Talador," he murmured, and the cowman stared at him. Drake arose, "Show me the one you got tied on the mule."

All three of them went outside. It was dark enough so that most of the townsmen who were strolling in the bland night did not notice anything on the mule standing patiently at the tie-rack out front of the jailhouse.

The large man went back there and lifted the dead man's head by the hair. Ben and Jeff looked. So did Drake Haslett. All any of them were certain about was that the dead man had been an Indian.

Ben jerked a thumb over his shoulder. "Drake; go fetch Lem Steele out here. He'd know."

While the sheriff was gone Ben introduced himself and Jeff, and the large young man said his name was Charley Gorman. He also said he ran cattle south and south-east of town. While he was saying this Jeff and Ben exchanged a glance. This was the man Drake was jealous of because he too had been paying court to the Sansouci woman. But right at this time none of that seemed very important, even though it probably had something to do with the obvious stiff backs when Drake and Charley Gorman met.

Drake returned shoving Lem Steele in front. The lawman from Verde Wells went over where Gorman was standing and did not even attempt to look at the dead man's face. He looked at the pair of carved— and empty—sixgun holsters, at the Apache moccasins below the embroidered *charro* trousers, and at the dangling dark hands with rings on each finger, then he turned away.

But Charley Gorman lifted the Apache's head and growled. "Take long look," he said. "Take a *damned* long look. You better be right when you answer, too. Is this Talador?"

Steele looked, turned his back to Gorman to face Drake, and nodded his head. "That's Talador," he quietly said, and moved back towards the doorway of the jailhouse.

Drake returned his prisoner to the cell-room while Ben finished the smoke he'd made inside, and dumped it to be tramped underfoot as he said, "Jeff; you reckon we'd ought to clean up?"

Ben had in mind a few drinks at the saloon but as filthy and offensive as they were it was very possible that they would be ushered out before they could get a drink.

Jeff said, "We got a bottle out at the canvas-camp."

Ben nodded and without a word to Charley Gorman, who watched, they turned southward and went hiking in the direction of the liverybarn. They still did not have their own saddle-stock but the horses they had taken from the raiders would be good enough.

17

FREIGHTERS

They did not take the mules back with them, but paid
the liveryman to feed and grain the mules in the
morning and to make certain they had plenty of fresh
water.

They also mentioned the two horses which had been
stampeded the previous night during the brush with
the raiders, and the liveryman said he would keep an
eye peeled. He asked where Sheriff Haslett had left
his horse, since the liveryman had seen him return to
town riding an Indian mount, and Ben impassively
said Drake Haslett's horse was back up the river two
or three miles, and let it go at that.

He and Jeff rigged out the same Apache animals
they had ridden to town. Ben shook his head over the
ornate *charro* saddle but said nothing as they left
town up the north alley and busted out into a lope
when they had Lincoln's lights behind them.

They were careful when they got up within the
vicinity of the camp, and although there was no
reason to believe any danger still existed, it was never

possible to approach a place where a deadly fight had taken place, particularly on a moonless night, without feeling something.

They dismounted north of the camp, led their horses into the trees up there, and very quietly walked down through, until they had the camp in full view. There, they remained in silent consideration of the wagon, the camp itself, the canvas-rooftop, for a while, then decided it was safe to do so, and walked forth.

Immediately three racoons caught their scent, which was not very difficult, and fled in all directions, upsetting two pans and a pot in their haste. The noise brought two cocked Colts out and up in seconds.

Jeff said, " 'Coons; I just saw two of the little camp-robbers high-tailing it."

They took care of the Indian horses, hobbled them and set them free to meander and graze. Ben said, "You'd ought to hide that Mex saddle. It's pretty damned garish."

Jeff puckered up. "It's what?"

"Too fancy with silver and all, and that horn bigger'n a man's hat."

Jeff shrugged. "Beats hell out of riding bareback," he said, and flung the *charro* saddle under the canvas-topped campsite, then kicked out of his boots, flung away his hat and dug in a warbag for a towel and a chunk of lye-soap. "Two lousy baths in the same day, and you know what—that lousy river is going to be cold."

Ben agreed. "Not just cold, but you taken a bath that often and my grandpaw used to say that's what makes folks' skin get wrinkled."

"Oh hell; it only gets wrinkled if you soak in the water. Even then those wrinkles go away."

"Yeah, but they come back. My grandpaw used to

say you could soak a person and look at him and you'd
see exactly what he'd look like in maybe twenty-five,
or thirty, years."

Jeff stood up in his shirt and trousers and stocking
feet and stared. "You believe that crap?"

Ben evaded a direct answer. "You've seen how
wrinkly some folks are, haven't you?"

"Oh for Chris'sake," muttered Jeff in monumental
disgust, and strode towards the river, towel over one
shoulder, bar of lye-soap in his hand.

Ben laughed to himself, shed his clothes and climbed
into his blankets. He also needed a bath, but not badly
enough, he told himself, to go down there in the dark
and bathe in water that was both cold and the colour
of ink.

He smoked a final cigarette while lying under the
canvas and waiting for all the tightness to leave his
nerves and muscles. It had been one hell of a twenty-
four hours. He recalled being warned against camping
up here because of the imminence of raiders; he also
remembered who had given him that warning.

He remembered a lot of things and as his eyelids
began to feel as though there were granules of sand
under each one, he punched out the smoke, groaned
mightily as he turned up on to his side, and went to
sleep long before Jeff returned blue and shivering, but
clean, to also bed down.

In the morning they heated extra water and shaved
—and swore fiercely because with that much of a
whisker-growth shaving was torture. Also, Ben had to
go down to the riverbank to bathe and the water was
colder this morning than it had been last night.

Later, they ate and looked at one another, found
nothing unusual except that both of them had lost
some weight and looked slightly gaunt in the face,

and both of them were cleaner now than they normally were, attired in fresh clothing and having scrubbed down twice.

Jeff said, "Let's go get the mules, see if anyone has found our horses yet, and get the hell out of here. If I never seen Lincoln again I won't feel at all bad."

Ben was willing. They killed time though, cleaning up after breakfast and going out to fetch back the rag-head horses. It was a magnificent day with a slight, high overcast to mitigate the morning heat which was rising even before they left the camp for town, and a mile on down the pike they saw a top-buggy coming smartly towards their camp at a swift trot. Ben squinted, then groaned.

"Haslett," he said, "and a woman."

He was right. Drake was freshly shaved and wearing a clean shirt when he hauled up at the side of the road and saluted the unsmiling pair of riders. The woman at his side was quite handsome, with just the faintest hint of grey in the wavy hair of her temples, but a face as smooth and unlined as the face of a girl.

Drake managed the introductions very well. Both Ben and Jeff raised their disreputable hats as Drake said, "Honey, these here are the men who helped me run down Talador and his crew."

Mrs. Sansouci looked at Ben, then at Jeff, with frank curiosity, then mechanically smiled.

They both smiled back just as mechanically and faced Drake with expressions of quiet reproach, but evidently in the company of the very handsome woman Sheriff Haslett noticed nothing but Mrs. Sansouci.

That was understandable; she was something that seemed to increase in beauty as people stood gazing at her. Ben's face mirrored a somewhat dolorous expression, as though while he might appreciate all that beauty, he felt reproachful towards himself because Mrs. Sansouci really did not impress him as anything but a beauty. Now a good, big stout young mule. . . .

"They got your horses at the liverybarn," stated Drake, cutting across Ben's thoughts. "Drifted in this morning." Drake looked a little critically at the Mex saddle Jeff was riding, and at the faded clothing of both freighters. "Well, we got to be getting along," he said, and saluted with his hand, which was encased in a fine buck-stitched roping glove of split buckskin.

Jeff and Ben turned to watch the rig go hastening on up the road. Jeff wrinkled his nose. "Was that Drake had that French toilet water on, or the woman? Smelt like one of those houses they got down in Mexico where. . . ."

"Never mind where you run across that smell of lavender before," broke in Ben, turning his horse back in the direction of town. "Did you hear what he said? We're the fellers who helped him catch Talador?"

Jeff had heard. "Like I already said, Ben, if I never got to set up another camp around Lincoln it will suit me just fine."

They resumed their way through the slightly hazy springtime morning with the 'feel' of oncoming summer in the soft, pleasant atmosphere, and far off to the east and west there was an increasing mistiness which could be presaging rainfall, or it could simply mean that more heat was on the way. In either case the pair of freighters were not especially bothered; they were accustomed to whatever weather Nature sent along. It was a hard life, but there had always been men who preferred it—providing they did not have to go after stolen mules too many times, and risk getting killed in the bargain.

Dell Bestsellers

- [ ] **SHARKY'S MACHINE** by William Diehl $2.50 (18292-1)
- [ ] **EVERGREEN** by Belva Plain $2.75 (13294-0)
- [ ] **WHISTLE** by James Jones $2.75 (19262-5)
- [ ] **A STRANGER IS WATCHING**
  by Mary Higgins Clark $2.50 (18125-9)
- [ ] **SUMMER'S END** by Danielle Steel $2.50 (18418-5)
- [ ] **MORTAL FRIENDS** by James Carroll $2.75 (15789-7)
- [ ] **THE BLACK MARBLE**
  by Joseph Wambaugh $2.50 (10647-8)
- [ ] **MY MOTHER/MY SELF** by Nancy Friday $2.50 (15663-7)
- [ ] **SEASON OF PASSION** by Danielle Steel $2.25 (17703-0)
- [ ] **BAD BLOOD** by Barbara Petty $2.25 (10438-6)
- [ ] **THE SEDUCTION OF JOE TYNAN**
  by Richard Cohen $2.25 (17610-7)
- [ ] **GREEN ICE** by Gerald A. Browne $2.50 (13224-X)
- [ ] **THE TRITON ULTIMATUM**
  by Laurence Delaney $2.25 (18744-3)
- [ ] **AIR FORCE ONE** by Edwin Corley $2.50 (10063-1)
- [ ] **BEYOND THE POSEIDON ADVENTURE**
  by Paul Gallico $2.50 (10497-1)
- [ ] **THE TAMING** by Aleen Malcolm $2.50 (18510-6)
- [ ] **AFTER THE WIND** by Eileen Lottman $2.50 (18138-0)
- [ ] **THE ROUNDTREE WOMEN: BOOK I**
  by Margaret Lewerth $2.50 (17594-1)
- [ ] **TRIPLE PLATINUM** by Stephen Holden $2.50 (18650-1)
- [ ] **THE MEMORY OF EVA RYKER**
  by Donald A. Stanwood $2.50 (15550-9)
- [ ] **BLIZZARD** by George Stone.........................$2.25 (11080-7)
- [ ] **THE DARK HORSEMAN**
  by Marianne Harvey $2.50 (11758-5)

At your local bookstore or use this handy coupon for ordering:

DELL BOOKS
P.O. BOX 1000, PINEBROOK, N.J. 07058

Please send me the books I have checked above. I am enclosing $_____
(please add 75¢ per copy to cover postage and handling). Send check or money
order—no cash or C.O.D.'s. Please allow up to 8 weeks for shipment.

Mr/Mrs/Miss _____

Address _____

City _____ State/Zip _____

SHARKY'S MACHINE

WILLIAM DIEHL

THE MOST SENSATIONAL THRILLER OF THE YEAR!

For Sharky, a hard-driving cop, it all begins as a routine Vice Squad assignment. Until he listens to the shocking, erotic tapes that send him searching for a call girl known as Domino. And what began as a job, becomes an obsession. "COMPELLING. THE COMPLETE THRILLER."—*Newsweek*

A Dell Book $2.50

At your local bookstore or use this handy coupon for ordering:

Dell	**DELL BOOKS** SHARKY'S MACHINE $2.50 (18292-1)
	P.O. BOX 1000, PINEBROOK, N.J. 07058

Please send me the above title. I am enclosing $_____
(please add 75¢ per copy to cover postage and handling). Send check or money order—no cash or C.O.D.'s. Please allow up to 8 weeks for shipment.

Mr/Mrs/Miss_____

Address_____

City_____ State/Zip_____

THE TRITON ULTIMATUM
by Laurence Delaney

The terrifyingly unforgettable story about the mysterious disappearance of the newest, biggest, deadliest weapons platform in history! Ten desperate men have brutally commandeered a Triton sub and 24 Poseidon missiles, more than enough to raze the world! They demand 4 billion in gold. But not even a golden ransom can save every major city on the globe once they make THE TRITON ULTIMATUM!   A Dell Book $2.25   (18744-3)

At your local bookstore or use this handy coupon for ordering:

Dell	**DELL BOOKS** **P.O. BOX 1000, PINEBROOK, N.J. 07058**	The Triton Ultimatum $2.25 (18744-3)

Please send me the above title. I am enclosing $_____
(please add 75¢ per copy to cover postage and handling). Send check or money order—no cash or C.O.D.'s. Please allow up to 8 weeks for shipment.

Mr/Mrs/Miss_____

Address_____

City_____ State/Zip_____

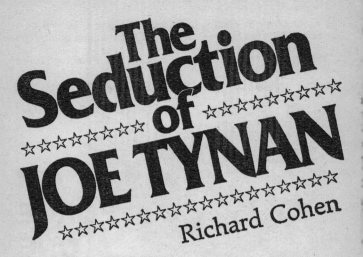

The Seduction of JOE TYNAN

Richard Cohen

A POWERFUL NEW FILM FROM UNIVERSAL STARRING ALAN ALDA.

Joe Tynan is a prominent U.S. Senator—a successful, young idealistic man who loves his wife and family. But as his stature and power grow, he finds that he must make a painful choice— between his career and his home life. The prize was power, but the price was everything he had.

A Dell Book $2.25

At your local bookstore or use this handy coupon for ordering:

| **Dell** | **DELL BOOKS**
 P.O. BOX 1000, PINEBROOK, N.J. 07058 | THE SEDUCTION OF JOE TYNAN $2.25
 (17610-7) |

Please send me the above title. I am enclosing $_____
(please add 75¢ per copy to cover postage and handling). Send check or money order—no cash or C.O.D.'s. Please allow up to 8 weeks for shipment.

Mr/Mrs/Miss_____

Address_____

City_____ State/Zip_____

A novel of terror aboard the President's plane, as one desperate man holds the passengers and crew at gun point, high
over the skies of America!
"The right ingredients. A top notch yarn."   *Pittsburgh Press*

A harrowing flight to the brink of disaster!

AIR FORCE ONE

by Edwin Corley
author of *Sargasso*

A Dell Book $2.50

(10063-1)

At your local bookstore or use this handy coupon for ordering:

Dell	**DELL BOOKS** **P.O. BOX 1000, PINEBROOK, N.J. 07058**	Air Force One $2.50 (10063-1)	

Please send me the above title. I am enclosing $ _____
(please add 75¢ per copy to cover postage and handling). Send check or money
order—no cash or C.O.D.'s. Please allow up to 8 weeks for shipment.

Mr/Mrs/Miss_____

Address_____

City_____ State/Zip_____